'As far as the eye can s[...]side is in bloom with [...] upon regiment are mounting as if to capture the sun. They are like a tide – a sea of scarlet waves, flecked with silver, brass, white and blue. A rich and splendid company, and none more so than the drummer boy.

'He marches there, raising his drumsticks almost haughtily as he thunders out the Advance. His eyes are bright and he smiles triumphantly as tall men grin and nod and secretly wave: for he is well-liked . . . being young, sturdy and full of hope.'

But a moment later the sound of Charlie Samson's drum was swallowed in a wilder thunder. The glorious scarlet troops had been ambushed. Men were dead and dying all around, and all the beauty was gone.

Hours later, the hillside quiet and still, Charlie came to himself again, his head fairly boiling with pain. All that was left of that fine army was himself and his drum and a few shady nightwalkers, cowards who came crawling from ditches and knaves who scoured the dead for wealth. Outwardly he was still the shining golden, hopeful lad, but all around him for many a day Charlie was to see human weakness, human pride and sloth and greed, and all the darkness that lay hidden in the management of that great army, until at last he found a way to lay his ghosts and build his life anew.

This is a sobering, haunting book, telling how one young man passes, as we all do, from the world of childhood dreams into the saddening world where adult failings and suffering are visible all around; but even in the sadness there lies a gleam of hope – for we cannot *be* disappointed unless somewhere there still remains within us the gleam of our former bright ideals.

Other books by Leon Garfield which are published in the Puffin series (not Peacocks) are *Jack Holborn*, *Smith*, *Black Jack*, *Mister Corbett's Ghost* and *Devil-in-the-Fog*.

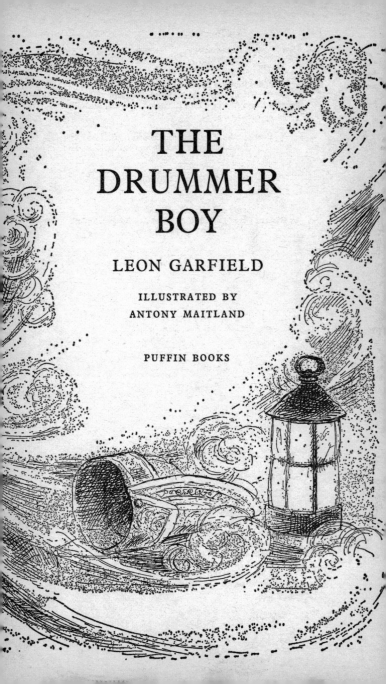

THE DRUMMER BOY

LEON GARFIELD

ILLUSTRATED BY
ANTONY MAITLAND

PUFFIN BOOKS

Puffin Books *A Division of Penguin Books Ltd,*
Harmondsworth, Middlesex, England
Penguin Books Australia Ltd, Ringwood, Victoria, Australia

—

First published by Longman Young Books 1970
Published in Peacock Books 1973

—

Copyright © Leon Garfield, 1970

—

Made and printed in Great Britain
by Richard Clay (The Chaucer Press) Ltd Bungay, Suffolk
Set in Monotype Plantin

To Vivien

THE DRUMMER
BOY

I

As far as the eye can see, scarlet men are marching. The hillside is in bloom with them. Regiment upon regiment are mounting as if to capture the sun.

There is a sound of drumming in the air that alarms the birds so that they wheel and flutter higher and higher till they are no more than black spots on the complexion of the sky.

They have risen from a wood that crowns the western side of the hilltop. It is not very large, this wood, but singularly dark; and under the sun it casts a sharp black shadow before it – like a pit.

Now comes a breeze that flutters the advancing pennants and briskens the glinting lines. They are like a tide – a sea of scarlet waves, flecked with silver, brass, white and blue. A rich and splendid company; and none more so than the drummer boy.

He marches there, raising his drumsticks almost haughtily as he thunders out the Advance. His eyes are bright and he smiles triumphantly as tall men grin and nod and secretly wave: for he is well-liked . . . being young, sturdy and full of hope.

Perhaps he struts a little, but no one minds. The drummer boy is their golden lad and he's caught the rhythm of their hearts.

It is to this rhythm that they march, and the drummer boy has the strange feeling that the shining regiments, rising and falling with a regular rustling thump as their black boots tread the grass, are the obedient spirits of his drum.

It is the grandest moment of his brief life. He glances up, as if to challenge the heavens to show anything finer than the glory mounting the hillside.

Then, of a dreadful sudden, the sound of his drum is swallowed up. A wilder thunder obscures it. The air seems to crumple into shreds and tatters as a storm of invisible iron rips through it. They have been ambushed!

The wood – the quiet wood – has changed most hideously. Red and orange pricks have sprouted all over it till it resembles some huge mad porcupine. Scarlet men begin to topple and fall with iron in their hearts.

But still the others march, rising and falling in close formation, as if the buzzing musket balls are no more than gnats.

Where is the drummer boy now? Quite transfixed with terror and awe he marches on as grown men crash about him bearing crimson medals on their scarlet chests. His life seems charmed; and to many his fierce young face and shining drum are the last sight of all.

Now little suns seem to burst at the wood's edge – and violent thunderclaps shake the air. Flowers of smoke blossom among the regiments – and leave emptiness behind.

And still the regiments come on. Their courage is supernatural; but their bodies are not. Some fifty yards from the hilltop there seems to be a toppling point that none can pass. Upright they come, then down they tumble, quite harvested.

The drummer boy – the drummer boy! Suddenly smoke obscures him. Following hearts contract. The smoke clears. Hearts beat again – he is not hit. A miracle. Again the smoke swirls; his buttons glint briefly – then vanish. This time he does not appear again. The proud drummer boy has fallen at last.

The hillside was quiet again. The smoke and dust had settled, and in their place a mist seeped down the slope, rendering the ground uneasy and indistinct. Little by little an enormous midnight swallowed up the sky – and all colour sank to black. The very hill seemed bandaged up in crepe.

Here and there broken wheels stood up – like spoked headstones in a graveyard of dreams; but otherwise shadows and

substance so intermingled that nothing was for certain. It was a strange and sombre landscape.

Suddenly there was a movement – a small stirring some threequarters the way up the hillside. There was a sharp cry of pain. A figure rose up. It staggered as if dazed . . . then it stood to a full height. It was the drummer boy; he was quite alone.

His face was deathly pale, save where it was painted with blood: there was a lump among his dusty hair the size of a small pudding – fetched up by a clout from a musket stock – and it fairly boiled with pain.

He looked about. He could see little, but the darkling air had a burnt out stink. Briefly he feared he'd been done for and had gone where the parson always said he would.

'Kippered, Charlie Samson. You're a dead 'un . . .' Then sense got the better of philosophy. 'No you ain't.' He saw he was the only soul left alive among a windfall of dead.

As his eyes grew accustomed to the dark, he saw them, shape upon shape lying quietly under the surface of the veiling mists. Broken muskets, standards, swords and tangled pennants lay with them – like remnants of some gigantic wreck. Then he saw something that gave him a sad pleasure: his drum. It had fallen and rolled some yards down the hill. He walked cautiously towards it, stared at it, shook his head over its dents. But it, like him, had come through with a whole skin. He picked it up and hitched it on.

Once more he was the drummer boy – the golden lad of the scarlet men – the sturdy young keeper of hope.

The drumsticks were still hanging from cords about his wrists. He gripped them and began to tap – tap softly. On such a night, in such a place it made a ghostly sound. His heart filled to overflowing with memories of the morning – and he fancied he heard once more the rustling thump of boots in the grass. In his mind's eye he saw again the hosts of smiling faces and discreet wavings moving ever upward towards that sudden bonfire where all their courage was burnt out.

To his surprise, he found himself to be marching, stalking

down the hillside, raising his drumsticks with all his old haughtiness. What was he playing? The Retreat. Slow and heavy, he was thundering out the Funeral Retreat for the glory fallen in the grass.

'God rest you all in peace . . .'

Down, down the hillside he came; and with him came the mist, floating knee-high. Now it met opposing currents in the lower air and eddied strangely about the lonely drummer boy. It lifted and fell – and gave him brief glimpses of more and more quiet shapes in the grass.

The mist seemed to tug and pluck at them, shifting torn facings and broken epaulettes as if they were the pennants of a second battle being fought again by the phantoms of the scarlet men. Here and there thick condensations plummeted quietly down – to rise again in vague blossoms, like the ghosts of the morning's cannon balls.

The drummer boy's heart grew cold. He was drumming now as much to keep up his own spirits as to pay homage to those of the dead.

'Keep a hold on yourself, Charlie Samson! There ain't nothing here but the fallen! Keep a hold on yourself now!'

He broke into a run and his shabby knees, striking the underside of his drum, provoked a deep thudding like the beating of a monstrous heart.

A wind had sprung up and was stirring the mists into more and more uncanny shapes so that they seemed to be rising out of the dead like spectres to the call of the drum.

His thoughts rushed back – no longer to the morning, but to the home he'd left behind; a warm, noisy inn in distant Lyndhurst, over the sea. Most deeply he wished he was there – even in the swill room. Wretchedly he recalled the angry pride in which he'd left it . . . and the haughty contempt with which he'd spent the King's Shilling in a rival house – to spite a family most negligent of their youngest son.

But wherever his thoughts flew he could not follow. There was no escape from the hillside.

'Rest in peace – rest in peace!' sobbed the drummer boy. *'For God's sake,* rest in peace!'

But God, it seemed, had forsook His office. There could be no more doubt. Out of the obscure dark they were coming, silently wading the mist. Gaunt and sombre shapes . . . flapping, limping, stumbling. Vague of aspect; part pitiful, part menacing – like moths to a candle, they were coming to the sound of the drum!

The drummer boy gave a violent groan. He rattled and thundered away like a soul possessed. He was unable to stop – till one spectral soldier, lean and grim in the uniform of the Twenty-third Foot, shambled across his path and seized him by the waist!

'For pity's sake,' the soldier roared above the din, 'give over that bleedin' row!' He grinned. 'Finch,' he said. 'By the grace of God a corporal and surviving.'

The drummer boy stopped. Amazement and joy shone in his eyes, as a helpless, happy smile spread over his face. A living man! Thank God – a living man!

Corporal Finch sniffed. Respectfully he edged a dead man with his boot; then went on earnestly: 'Being horse-de-combat on account of a twisted ankle honourably come by in the baggage train, I ain't quite oh-fay with the forchuns of war. In a word, young gent, 'oo won?'

In the fallen silence that followed, the corporal's companions drew near. Three peep-eyed privates half sepulchred in twigs and leaves and dust. Even Charlie Samson, young as he was, had come to know such gentlemen as these survivors. The shifty, creeping rag-bag of the Quartermaster's and the Paymaster's and the Baggagemaster's spearhead of attack. The warriors who diced, not so much with death as with each other in every nook and hole and cranny they could find; and whose worst enemy was the sergeant who winkled them out. The dust and twigs that now bedecked them were but remembrances of the ditch in which they'd hid while the battle had raged.

The drummer boy stared at them in bewilderment. Corporal Finch leaned forward and scraped a grubby finger across the drum to fetch Charlie out of his dream.

'Went the day well, young 'un? Did our arms prosper? Was we victorious, so to speak?'

'I – I don't know,' muttered the drummer boy, his head aching vilely and his spirit suddenly oppressed.

'Come, come, lad!' said the corporal kindly. 'You was there right in the middle of it, wasn't you? In among the blood and what-not, eh? You must have seen which way our companions de la gurr hoofed it?'

But it turned out that no more than Corporal Finch did Charlie know which side had died in vain. The outcome of the battle remained as mysterious as the desolate night itself.

The corporal shrugged his shoulders. 'You'd best keep with us, then – while we finish doing what we can for the glorious mort.' He laid his hand quite tenderly on Charlie's sleeve; and for a moment the drummer boy was revived into thinking better of the gaunt corporal and his band.

Then with the golden lad among them, these scarlet men (who wore their scarlet with a difference) went back to the task the sound of the drum had broken off.

'La mort came quick and sudden to our poor countrymen,' murmured the corporal, as he stalked inquisitively through the dark. 'They was unready. Unshriven, you might say. Affairs left pitiful and unfinished. So we, the quick, so to speak, can 'elp the dead, God bless 'em. Letters might come our way whose business we can 'appily conclude. Call it a charity – Aha! A capitaine! Stand back, mon ammies – he's mine!'

The dead captain lay with his chest pressed to the ground and his face turned sideways. His mouth was open, so that it seemed that 'la mort' – in the shape of a musket ball clean through him – had arrested him in the very act of taking a giant mouthful of grass. Patiently he submitted to the corporal's search.

'Bills . . . bills,' muttered Finch. 'Mon Dew, but la mort did this one a favour.' The corporal shook his head and pocketed up the captain's watch, snuffbox, gold ring and several coins. Then he turned the dead man over and endeavoured to close his eyes and fix his hands across his breast.

'Two birds with one stone,' he explained. 'Out of respect and to mark 'em as having been done, so to speak.'

'Any luck, Corp?' called a tall soldier with fair hair who was rifling the pockets of another of the dead.

'Mustn't grumble, Parsons.'

But Parsons did. It seemed he never had any luck. His gentlemen seemed to have gone to meet their maker woefully unprepared. Never so much as a bleeding brass farthing . . .

So they went on; the boy, with his drum, trudging wretchedly beside the lean and grim figure of Corporal Finch who talked and robbed and talked and robbed and filled the air with the familiar homely stink of gin and rum.

By now there were tears running down Charlie Samson's scratched and filthy cheeks. But they were not tears for the dead whose grey faces in the grass seemed no more than dull mementoes. They were tears for an enterprise collapsed. The bright blazing dream of battle and grandeur had coldly clouted him on the head and returned him – no more than slightly damaged – to a grubby world he thought he'd escaped. To Corporal Finch and his band. In his heart of hearts he knew that his companions of the moment were the companions of all his life. They were brothers to his brothers and to all he'd ever known. Through no fault of his own, the golden lad wore a tarnished air.

From time to time the corporal, who seemed to regard him as a shining mascot, offered him little pilfered keepsakes; but the drummer boy shrank from them . . .

The wind grew stronger and blew off the high clouds. One by one the stars broke out and the landscape grew in all its solemn particulars. Dark and scowling, the hilltop rose behind them, and the wood crowned it like a judge's cap.

But most striking of all was the motion of the mists. The wind was rolling them back like a tremendous dust sheet under which there seemed to be lying a great dormitory of gentlemen murdered in their beds.

This sight put new life into the survivors who hastened to and fro, flapping down like buttoned birds among the tumbled sleepers; but the drummer boy's heart almost broke.

'Watch out, Charlie,' said the corporal abruptly, and gripped his arm.

In the grass at his feet lay a young soldier. The starlight lent him a silvery air that was coldly beautiful. He was half covered by a tattered flag – as if he'd pulled it across himself to keep out the eternal chill.

'La mort,' sighed the corporal. 'La cruel mort.' Then he turned away to pastures less green.

But the drummer boy stayed. Almost enviously the golden lad stared down on the silver youth.

Suddenly he saw, clutched in the outflung right hand, a scrap of paper. He knelt down . . . and Corporal Finch observed him with a touch of wry amusement.

It was a letter. The drummer boy's heart quickened. Gently he took the crumpled paper and spread it out. He read slowly, for the stars gave a poor light and his own schooling wasn't much stronger. (His father, the Lyndhurst innkeeper, held that an ale tally was all his youngest had need to read.) But the letter proved simple and the words direct.

To be given into the hand of Sophia Lawrence of Bruton Street, London, with the news of the death in battle of James Digby who loved her with all his heart and all his soul and all his might. Tell her he died bravely and that his last prayer was for God to bless her and keep her well.

As he read, the present circumstance faded from the drummer boy's mind. Once more the scarlet men were on the march as this letter from across the grave linked life to death and death to life.

'I'll tell her, James Digby,' he whispered. 'I promise you that.'

For minutes he stood there, gazing blindly into the night

while the four soldiers spread out and went about their unholy business. Suddenly he became aware that a fifth figure had appeared. A shortish, stout man who waddled towards Corporal Finch with anxious wavings and faint cries. The corporal seemed to know him. They greeted each other ... and the corporal pointed back towards the drummer boy.

'Charlie!' came his voice; but the drummer boy remained where he was, like a sentinel over the young soldier. So the corporal and the newcomer came to Charlie.

' 'Ere 'e is, Mister Shaw, sir! Charlie Samson. Late of the valley of the shadder, as you might say. The warrior lad 'imself.'

Mister Shaw was grey and fat, with little, frightened eyes. He shook Charlie by the hand. His grip was surprisingly firm. 'Pleased to make the acquaintance, my dear.'

He was a surgeon. Charlie smiled sadly. Not much for a surgeon hereabouts.

'Don't you believe it,' said Corporal Finch proudly. 'La mort ain't the end for our Mister Shaw. Tell 'im, sir – tell 'im what's in them two little bags.'

So Mister Shaw told him; and the drummer boy shuddered to the depths of his soul. The surgeon had been gathering teeth. Fine, fresh teeth. Teeth for the toothless back home. Teeth for the ladies; teeth for the gentlemen – at upwards of two pound ten a gnasher. In his two little leather bags – that rattled as he shook them – the surgeon judged he'd close on two hundred guineas ...

'Stand back, my dear!' Mister Shaw had spied the silver youth at Charlie's feet. 'Stand aside.'

'No! No! Not him!' The drummer boy's eyes burned with a sudden fury. Fiercely he raised his drumstick and stood over the fallen soldier. The surgeon stared at him in bewilderment; then he gave a little bleating laugh.

'He – he! Did you think I was after his teeth, my dear?'

'Then – what?'

'I was going to see what could be done. He's still alive, y'know ...'

Alive?'

Almost fearfully the drummer boy looked down. The young soldier was moving! His eyes were opening. 'Alive . . .' The drummer boy breathed the word as if anything louder might put out the delicate flicker in the grass. He backed away. The young soldier turned his head. His eyes, now wider, met Charlie Samson's. Silently they stared at each other. A strange moment.

The surgeon was kneeling. He was asking the young man where he was hit. The young man seemed not to understand.

'Your wound. Where? Where?'

Somehow the news spread to the busy robbers. They came quickly; gathered round. They were pleased – even delighted. They stared and grinned. Anyone would think they'd never seen a living man before. Anyone would think that the little flicker the surgeon tended and the drummer boy guarded was more precious than anything else to be found on the hillside.

And Charlie Samson forgave the fat, unpleasant surgeon all his gruesome sins if only his skill should prove sufficient. He held his breath.

But there was no need. The fallen soldier – James Digby of the tragic letter and the deathless love – was in no immense danger.

It turned out that when the first shot had been fired, he'd gone down like a sack of miserable oats. And stayed down till the last shot had echoed and died away. Then – quite overcome by the murderous tumult through which he'd quaked, he'd fallen asleep . . . dozed off with the flag to keep him warm.

The drummer boy turned away; he was sick at heart. This last seemed the cruellest blow of all. The world collapsed about him in dingy stinking ruins. All that was bright and shining had perished. Only the rubbish remained. Finch and his three followers; the unwholesome Mister Shaw – and now James Digby, who had seemed the inmost spirit of the scarlet men with his love that bridged the grave.

'Why ain't you dead?' he muttered; and he stared bleakly at

the young soldier who returned his look with the most amiable smile in the world.

'Friends!' Coporal Finch's voice. It had an uneasy edge. His followers gathered. There was an alarmed look on his large, somewhat bird-like face. 'Mister Shaw 'as just given me a piece of un'appy news. Forchun frowned on our enterprise. Our valour 'as been 'umbled, as you might say. In a word, gents, we lost and we'd best 'oof it bleedin' quick!'

Fear spread like a disease from face to face; but military habit made them attend the corporal. The coast. They must get to the coast. It was their only hope. The sea – a ship – and the homeland for which they'd fought.

The scarlet men were abandoned as if they'd been red hot; and the seven survivors set off. Corporal Finch led, while James Digby and the drummer boy fetched up the rear. No one looked back – not even Charlie Samson.

Presently the shambling shapes dissolved into the night. Only a faint, regular thud could be heard as Charlie's over-large drum struck against his knee. Then this too died away and the battlefield lay quiet and forsaken. Only the wind whispered and stroked the long grass across dead faces – as if to cross them out.

Then, perhaps ten minutes later, there was a movement. It began in the dark and terrible wood. A shadow seemed to detach itself and flit weirdly down the hillside. It seemed to hop and leap at a great rate ... but made no sound. Down, down the hillside it came, rushing across the field as if pursued. But it was pursuing. It was pursuing Corporal Finch's band. It was, or seemed to be, the figure of a man ...

2

THEY blundered through the night. Such spirits as they had, they kept up with singing, cursing and quarrelling – save at the rear where James Digby and the drummer boy marched side by side. Charlie was quiet. A vague sense of being followed oppressed him, as if the scarlet men were drifting in their wake. But James Digby felt no such uneasiness. Instead, he whiled away the dark by opening his heart to the troubled drummer boy.

Like Charlie Samson he, too, was a youngest son. But there the resemblance ended. James Digby was a gentleman; and the drummer boy was not. Digby had gone to war to prove himself worthy of the lady he loved; Charlie had gone to find something to be worthy of. Neither of them had been particularly success-ful. But it was plain that James Digby's breeding stood him in good stead. He was able to put a brave face on his dismal cowardice and treat it as if it had never been.

Time and again the drummer boy marvelled at the power of a love that could have stuffed so flimsy a spirit into the glory of scarlet. But then Charlie Samson and love were not deeply acquainted. High-nosed kitchen maids had been the scope of inquiries and the top of his ambitions. He knew nothing of a general's gleaming daughter (the very general who had com-manded the fatal advance); for such was Sophia Lawrence of Bruton Street. Nor was there anything that James Digby could say that made her more real to the drummer boy than some vague dream.

But there was no doubt at all that Mister Shaw was fascin-ated. The wealth and importance of James Digby's connection brought out the worst in the portly surgeon. He buzzed about the slender gentleman like a fat fly, and fawned on the chance of an introduction. He sniggered at Digby's wit, sighed over his sentiment and hung perspiring on his lightest word. He was a bulging, horrible pig of a man . . . and Charlie Samson longed to push him into the black ditch that ran along the side of the road like a bereavement.

The surgeon seemed to sense the drummer boy's hostility and, from time to time, retired to the head of the band where the singing and cursing and quarrelling went ceaselessly on.

Corporal Finch's ankle still troubled him. He leaned first on docile Parsons, and then on another friend of his – Mushoo. Surprisingly, Mushoo turned out to be a Frenchman – an enemy, so to speak. They'd come upon each other in the self-same ditch while the battle raged apart. A look, a nod and a grin had been sufficient. They were of a kind. No less than the English, the French had their warriors of the Quartermaster's Stores.

If the corporal had an enemy in the world, it wasn't the Frenchman. Edwards, a short, pin-headed Welshman, seemed to have taken against him, most likely on account of some fancied slight. Full of Celtic bile, he sneered and jeered at the lofty corporal and his convenient limp. For a time the corporal

bore it patiently; then he began to turn very military and snapped off Edwards's head whenever that offensive object showed itself. But Edwards always grew another, more contemptuous than the last.

Little by little the night drained away and the road stretched bleakly before them, imprisoned between tall poplars for the term of its visible life. Nor was the sky more cheerful. Dark clouds were gathering in wisps and clots. They were joining and spreading, turning over and over as if troubled with bad dreams. Darker and darker they bulked till at last they stood in the sky like a huge black forest.

Uneasily the survivors peered up; then hastened on to escape the coming storm. But this was an ambush there was no avoiding. Suddenly a great claw of lightning reached across and tore the sky wide open. The heavens roared with pain; and the rain came down like musket balls.

The survivors cursed and fled. Shelter – shelter! The fields stretched dismally on either side. Neither house nor cottage nor any living thing was to be seen; and the air was in tatters under the fusillades of rain. Shelter – shelter! They stumbled on, streaming and gaping.

'Shelter!' Corporal Finch saw it. A barn, standing by itself not thirty yards off the road. It had a weird and abrupt air – as if it had been abandoned on being caught out in some crime. But it would hold off the rain.

They tumbled inside and lay panting while the rain thudded angrily and the roof groaned in distress. Then Edwards began again. He blamed the corporal for their plight; the lame and feeble leadership . . .

Corporal Finch, reclining between Parsons and Mushoo, let him have his say. Then he sat up.

'Sentry-go for you, mon share?'

'What?'

'You 'eard. Someone's got to watch over our slumbers. And 'oo better than crafty old you, mon share.'

Edwards clenched his fists; but the corporal, flanked by his friends, was unmoved. He smirked. 'What with being torchered with the 'orrors on my account, you wouldn't 'ave got much of a dormey anyways.'

So Edwards, outgeneraled and outnumbered, swore and took up a place by the ragged doorway. He leaned against it, and urged his weight with a malevolent air . . .

Corporal Finch went to sleep. His beaked face among the aged straw took on the grotesque innocence of a new hatched owl. Presently Parsons and Mushoo joined him, and the three of them lay in a peaceful buzzing heap while Edwards, watching the teeming rain, urged his weight still more against the doorway and thought his thoughts.

Mister Shaw was making James Digby comfortable. From time to time he caught the drummer boy's contemptuous eye, and looked briefly abashed. But it was plain that the silvery youth had more to offer than the one-time golden lad. He'd fastened himself on to Digby like an enormous leech. They would go to Bruton Street together. Companions in arms, ha – ha! He, Mister Shaw, had always had a great admiration for General Lawrence – it would be an honour to meet him, and his friends.

The surgeon fondled his bags of teeth, then gobbled on of the prosperous times that lay ahead, in gilded Bruton Street, for two such veterans from the hillside.

Vainly the drummer boy tried to shut them out – sometimes rattling his fingers on his drum, sometimes just staring out past leaning Edwards into the curtain of rain.

But the two veterans would not let him be. James Digby kept smiling at him – an odd, lopsided smile that gave him an attractive, goblin air.

He wanted the drummer boy to share in the thought of the wonderful days to come. He wanted the drummer boy to be dazzled by the brightness of Sophia. (As he spoke her name, a strange, almost lost look came into his eyes.) 'And here I am on my way back to her as if nothing had happened . . . as if it was all a dream, Charlie –'

Tears filled the drummer boy's eyes. His glorious men in scarlet were no more than a dream. A wild anger rose up in him. He tightened his fists and thrust them into his pockets to stop himself doing James Digby an injury.

A piece of paper met one of them. Puzzled, he took it out. It was James Digby's letter – the deathless love – the words that had called across the grave.

'Since – since you're on your way back,' he muttered, 'you can deliver this lousy rubbish yourself.' He screwed the letter into a ball and flung it into Digby's startled face.

Anxiously, apologetically, Mister Shaw picked it up and offered it to his gentleman friend. Digby took it. Smoothed it out; read – and grinned.

'Lord!' he said. 'It takes you back, don't it, Charlie!'

It did indeed. Once more the drummer boy saw the dark hillside and the butchered captain screaming quietly into the grass. And then like a mocking echo, the memory of his own feelings came back when he'd stood, staring down at the flag-shrouded silver youth. 'Why – for God's sake, why wasn't you really dead?' he whispered, wearied of a world that was so monstrously unjust. But there was no sinking James Digby with wishing.

He looked quite bewildered that anyone could wish him dead. Then the odd lost look flickered in his eyes.

'Sophia –' he began; but got no further. There was a terrible roar and a crash, together with several screams.

'Me arm! Me arm! Oh God, me arm!'

Whose arm? Where? Who was screaming? Filth, mud, splinters, bricks and rotting straw seemed to be flying everywhere. A wild confusion obscured everything. A wall had fallen and the roof had come in. Edwards – Edwards was screaming. 'Dear God, me arm's smashed!'

He lay amid a muddle of rubbish with his arm under the great beam that had supported the roof. Mister Shaw was by him. The others were struggling for themselves. All save one.

'Mister Shaw – over here, sir.' Charlie Samson pulled at him.

'What is it, my dear?'

'Over here, quick!'

The surgeon left moaning Edwards. He went with Charlie Samson. James Digby lay face down. The other end of the beam had struck the side of his head; and broken into it. He was stone dead. In his outstretched hand was clasped – with a terrible despairing grip – his letter. Mister Shaw gazed gloomily at his departed hope. 'Kippered,' he grunted, then went back to Edwards.

The damage to Edwards proved not severe. His left upper arm was snapped. A clean break, said Mister Shaw coolly, which was interesting as it was the only clean thing about him. Mister Shaw set the bone with almost feminine delicacy, and, though the Welshman bellowed like a bull, it was plain Mister Shaw never hurt him. As he worked at his trade, he was quite a different man from the fawning collector of teeth and rich acquaintances.

The terrible rain quenched any attempt to bury James Digby. 'But for the grass of Dew,' said Corporal Finch by way of an epitaph; then added, 'not that 'e was ever the surviving kind.' The survivors hastened away, gasping helplessly against the enmity of the sky.

Charlie Samson looked back. He was still dazed by the suddenness of the disaster. Once more in his pocket was the letter. For a second time he'd taken it from James Digby's outstretched hand. Did he mean to deliver it? God knew –

James Digby's tomb lay under the teeming rain. Not even two chance rafters had contrived to form a cross above it. It was a flattened ruin.

Suddenly Charlie fancied a movement . . . a touch of old scarlet. Then nothing. Ghosts . . . ghosts in his mind's eye. He shook his head and stumbled on.

3

FROM the hillside to the coast at Calais the torrent continued
to fall. The roads and fields were drowned; the ruined cottages,
the shattered barns and all the wide wreckage of war sank into
the providential mud as if God had decided He'd best begin
the world again. From the hillside to the coast at Calais every
living thing streamed and ran . . . save Corporal Finch and his
band of survivors who streamed and hobbled. Shelter – shelter!

But all was open to the sky; so, heavy with mud, they moved
on, on towards the distant sea.

They quarrelled no more. The disaster in the barn had
promoted a peace between the corporal and the wounded
Welshman. The corporal had a shrewd notion that Edwards
had provoked it out of spite. Consequently he looked to the
injured man with some respect. Enmity abated as understanding grew. The corporal granted full military consideration to
Edwards in his plight; and Edwards honoured him for it and
was quick to support his authority. They were now as united
a band as could be found anywhere in the king's uniform.

All save the drummer boy. He stalked apart in a lonely
despair . . . and the rain beat a grim tattoo on his drum. The
sense of being followed was stronger than ever. Time and
again he looked back; but the thick rain veiled the air and he
saw nothing for certain.

Mister Shaw was trying to make up to him. He'd seen him
take the letter. He was anxious to go to Bruton Street with him.
After all, who better than a surgeon to break the news of a
tragic loss? Together – the surgeon and the golden lad.

The drummer boy shook his head and brushed the surgeon
away. He preferred his loneliness . . .

'Shelter!'

A gun carriage and a powder waggon, helplessly locked together, lay abandoned in the road – probably to forestall pursuit. Gratefully the survivors heaved in under the waggon's canvas roof.

Sleep. All they wanted was to sleep. The corporal peered round. 'Sentry-go for you, mon share. Watch over us. Guard us from all trouble, sorrow and 'urt.'

This time he'd fixed on the warrior lad himself – who was nesting on his drum in the waggon's tail.

The drummer boy looked up. He nodded. He alone had no great desire to sleep. He feared his dreams . . .

The survivors huddled damply into corners, and, one by one, they mumbled off, sometimes taken in the middle of a word. Last to go was soaking Mister Shaw who'd offered to watch in Charlie's place. 'You need your beauty sleep . . . my dear . . . your . . . your eyes are – are – aah –' Then he, too, was gone the Lord knew where, and the drummer boy was alone to watch into the endless rain.

Down it whirled – the tiny silver artillery of the clouds – splintering in the mud and against the melancholy trees. Wearily he looked out, and tried with all his might to heave the image of James Digby out of his mind.

He stared at the tall trees till his eyes ached and his brain sang. But the rain kept whispering, 'Sophia . . . Sophia,' and the dead youth's last look gazed into his inner eye.

Suddenly he fancied a movement over behind one of the trees. Nothing much: seen out of the corner of his eye. A touch of red . . .

The drummer boy's hands reached for his drumsticks.

He leaned forward. Peered carefully. Nothing. He'd imagined it. The violence he'd endured had shaken phantoms awake in his brain. Nonetheless, he continued to watch the tree with immense care and concentration. 'Sophia . . . Sophia,' hissed the rain malevolently –

'Sophia!'

The drummer boy's heart jerked. Who'd spoken? One of the

sleepers behind him? He looked; observed them heaving gently, like a single beast with five blind heads.

Then had it been his own voice, repeating the whisper in the rain? He began to turn back.

His hands shook. The sense of someone watching was appallingly strong. Who was it? A figure, in scarlet coat, stood for a tiny instant beyond the edge of his eye. A face stared at him out of the rain. Lost eyes peered into his own; and the head was broken and bloody. Then it was gone – as if the rain had washed it away.

'James Digby!' screamed the drummer boy; and his trembling hands awoke the drum.

'Your eyes are wild, Charlie, wild!' mumbled Mister Shaw, coming out of his dream at the exact point he'd entered it.

Then everyone was awake in a panic. What had the drummer boy seen? The corporal seized him by the wrist – thrust his huge face close. What was it? How many? Speak up –

But there was nothing to be got from the white-faced sentry, who shook and shook his head. The corporal sighed and let go of his wrist. The warrior lad must have dropped off . . . even had a dream, and beaten his bleeding drum without rightly knowing what he was doing.

Attempts were made to return to sleep, but with no success. Though it was certain the overtired drummer boy had been alarmed by his own imagining, the abrupt awakening had done for the survivors' rest. Besides, they were monstrously hungry. Their bellies grunted and groaned.

So they left the shelter of the waggon and stumbled out into the streaming dusk. Once more they were on their journey towards the distant sea.

Sixty miles stretched before them. Sixty sodden miles. They tottered on. Now along the desolate road, now past farms and villages where nought seemed to remain but wild wet children, bewildered by the ruin of their inheritance. Savage eyes these children cast upon the dripping survivors as they passed, and screamed shrill curses after their backs. An army had passed that way and everywhere there was the stench of fires put out by the teeming rain.

They limped circumspectly through these places, between midnight and the dawn. They stole for their suppers; they stole for their breakfasts; they slept where they might – and moved painfully on: six of the wettest, filthiest objects that had ever crawled across the fair face of France.

But they had the golden lad among them; and sometimes, when the rain paused for breath, he tapped out a little march for them, and then they rose to almost human height.

He walked with a pale and inward air; but he did not walk alone. James Digby walked beside him. When he slept, James Digby lay beside him, with strange lost eyes and shattered head. The drummer boy was haunted, and he could not escape.

Sometimes the phantom was behind him, drifting with his shadow; sometimes it was whispering in his mind. Though he'd never seen it for certain since the day in the waggon, its presence filled the air. The letter . . . the letter . . . Charlie must deliver the letter. It seemed that the phantom would never rest till it was enthroned in a living heart –

'– With the news of the death in battle of James Digby.'

'But it wasn't so!'

'Tell her he died bravely –'

'It wasn't so!'

'And that his last prayer was for God to bless her and keep her well.'

'No – no –'

But Charlie struggled in vain. James Digby dead was stronger than ever he'd been alive. He was stronger, even, than the scarlet men . . .

As he remembered them, the ghost stared bleakly into his soul. Its bloody face was thin with envy. And then Charlie knew, with a prickle of dismay, that the phantom was an outcast. Never could it join the scarlet men – so long as the drummer boy barred its way.

'Tell her I died bravely . . .'
'But it wasn't so . . .'
'Tell her . . .'

The chief roads were becoming clogged with baggage wag-gons abandoned in the mud. More and more of these huge obstacles met the survivors in their path, till at last, on Mushoos advice, they struck off towards the south. Sooner or later they would reach the sea . . .

'That letter!' panted Mister Shaw, oozing along beside Charlie and finding the going hard. 'Best let me come along with you, my dear. After all, I knew him too!'

Palely the drummer boy stared at him, as if the words had been addressed to someone at his side. Mister Shaw frowned. He was not offended; it took a great deal to offend Mister Shaw. He was puzzled by the change in the boy. Nonetheless, he continued to pester him, for the golden lad had a key to the world that had always turned its face from Mister Shaw . . . and – and he'd grown fond of Charlie Samson, besides.

He did his best to stifle the latter reason as if he sensed that, sooner or later, it would bring him down. So this portly bundle of rubbish, stinking like an old cabbage, bounced and splashed beside the troubled drummer boy and talked and talked of Bruton Street, the General and the profits to be got from fine fresh teeth.

Then, quite suddenly, he tripped and fell. But he was up again in an instant, beaming like a portrait in mud. The drummer boy smiled back; and again the surgeon frowned. He did not like the drummer boy's smile. It struck a chill into his heart. It was an odd, lopsided smile that gave the drummer boy a curiously goblin air.

The fat man stared up at the dark sky as if he had an enemy there and muttered under his breath. For a little while after this he kept away from Charlie; but then he drifted back with a mournful fascination . . .

This was on May twenty-first: the tenth night of their journey. It was the night the survivors reached the sea.

The rain had all but perished, and the sky, worn threadbare, let the stars poke through. The air had a sharp salt edge.

They moved along a narrow rutted path that rose towards a clump of trees. All talk was stilled, and there was an expectancy in their approach. A sound was in the air: a sighing, muttering sound.

They reached the trees and stared out across the estates of the night. Before them, dark and still, with a faintly rippled sheen, was the sea.

They looked down. A huddle of cottages lay below; and a finger of the tide scratched at the shingle with a ragged silver nail.

Corporal Finch, like a seedy bird of prey, overhung the descent to see where best to pounce. Cracks and spots of light leaked out of one of the cottages; the rest were sleeping in their shadows. Several small boats lay upturned upon the beach. None of them drew the corporal. Instead his eyes glinted on a more substantial craft. A longboat lay closer to the water; and some forty yards beyond it a two-masted fishing vessel waited at anchor . . . like a parent for a reluctant child.

Thievery sprang first to the survivors' minds – being most at home there. Then caution. Though they were ready, willing and able to filch the longboat and then the fishing vessel, there wasn't one of them who'd the faintest notion which of the infernal muddle of ropes that festooned the ship to apply to for benefit of the wind. Without assistance, they were done.

The corporal's eyes returned to the gleaming cottage. Most likely it was an inn. The corporal grinned. He rubbed his claw-like hands together. What might not five fierce soldiers and a drummer boy persuade simple fisherfolk to do for them? Anything – so long as they left them their lives.

Menacingly he nodded and signalled a descent. They moved

down the steep path towards the unsuspecting inn like six malicious ghosts.

Some minutes after they'd left the clump of trees, something else took their place. It limped and flapped into the shadows and there remained. It was the figure of a man . . .

4

THE survivors crouched by the door of the inn. Their aspect was threatening and even savage. The corporal booted open the door and the light streamed out. Such had been the darkness and secrecy of their world that, for a moment, they stood help-lessly revealed, like a conspiracy of dazzled moths. Then they clumped inside – five fierce and filthy soldiers together with a drummer boy and his drum.

'Bonn swar!' roared the corporal, glaring round with a murderous grin.

Faces turned to stare at him: hard, sea-crackled faces, sour, stony faces, faces like old boots. A faint gleam of curiosity flickered from one to another, then lost itself in the shadows where it was finally put out.

Shadows. The parlour was well stocked with them – the first fine blaze of light diminishing into a smoky dinginess supplied by two lanterns.

'Bonn swar!' repeated the corporal; but the faces had all been extinguished in tankards and behind backs. 'Bleedin' 'eathens,' said Corporal Finch, and bade Mushoo parley with his stinking countrymen so they might oblige the survivors or suffer the consequence of war.

Mushoo stepped forward and, hands on hips, fired off a quantity of French like grapeshot. Corporal Finch attended carefully to scavenge what he could. If there was one thing the gaunt, bird-like corporal respected, it was a foreign tongue. Even in the desperate days of the journey he'd pecked at every mumble of Mushoo's – and thereafter dappled his own con-versation with his gleanings.

But all that Mushoo got out of his stinking countrymen was space made for a wizened potboy who came out of the gloom like a spider and asked if he might fetch wine.

What in God's name was to be done now? They sat at an empty table and Corporal Finch gazed round terribly at the swilling French pigs who stood between the survivors and home. For the first time the corporal and his band had cause to hate the French.

'And where was they when the battle raged?' he asked bitterly. 'That nut–faced fatty over there!' He jerked his head towards a little man with apple-cheeks and pin-sized eyes who watched him uncomprehendingly. 'If I'd 'ave met 'im on that field of blood I'd 'ave wrapped 'is guts around 'is neck!'

One by one, the corporal ripped the souls out of the silent fishermen and shredded them with his contemptuous tongue. Then the ancient potboy brought the wine and Mushoo paid. Crimson vinegar – but it helped. Once more they were the survivors, and survive they would! They'd prig the fishermen's bleeding boat! Somehow or another they'd find a way to sail it. The more wine they drank, the more confident they became. And the more cunning. The corporal dug Charlie in the ribs.

'Give us a tune, lad!'

'What?'

'Give us a rattle on your drum, Charlie. Just to cheer us up, eh?'

Charlie stared blankly at the grinning corporal. Finch explained: they needed the longboat. But to shove it over the shingle would be horribly noisy. The boozy pigs in the parlour would hear it: unless there was a louder noise to cover it. 'So just you make it thunder, Charlie . . . and that there military sound will be doing a power of good!'

Charlie Samson woke out of his eerie dreams. He stared about the parlour. He met surly indifference. His father's house in Lyndhurst had a grander parlour, but the homely air of homelessness – the fireside of eternal strangers – was the same.

'Parsons and Mushoo nip out first; and then –'

Charlie nodded. He fetched up his drumsticks from the top

of his boot and balanced them idly in his hands. Parsons and Mushoo . . . First he saw them, dozing against the wall. Then he saw them not. They might have melted into the air. Their going had been a miracle of discretion.

The corporal touched Charlie with his foot. His horny lidded eyes flickered. Now! Charlie's heart quickened. His hands trembled. Suddenly the survivors and their world depended utterly on him and his drum.

Softly he tapped on it. He saw Mister Shaw begin to sweat and force a smile. But the hard-faced fishermen remained unmoved. What was the sound of a drum to them?

Charlie frowned with concentration. He found a rhythm, a light and dancing rhythm. The wizened potboy, caught between the lanterns, had crossed shadows. He looked more like a spider than ever; all his legs seemed to be spinning a web. He was dancing . . .

Charlie fancied he heard the sound of a keel grinding on shingle. Desperately he rattled louder. Now the beat was lilting, a mocking cousin to the Advance.

Mister Shaw was watching him with fascination. An exultation began to fill the drummer boy. He seemed to be possessed by the spirit of the military drum. Now the Advance sounded over and across the dance, as if regiments were sweeping through gaiety. The parlour's lanterns shook and quivered, the walls seemed to dissolve and the drummer boy's head was flooded with sunshine and glitter as the regiments mounted the hillside. With all his old haughtiness he raised his drumsticks high; the golden lad. Up and up went the scarlet men . . .

Corporal Finch was clapping his hands and stamping his great feet in time; the spidery potboy was capering neatly – watching his countless feet admiringly. But the stony fishermen drank on, still unmoved by the wild young drummer boy who rattled away by the door.

Edwards had vanished . . . more secretly even than Parsons and Mushoo before him.

Charlie thundered on. His wrists were aching and he was

37

part blinded with sweat. It seemed he'd been playing for an hour. Dimly he saw the little apple-cheeked man watching him curiously. A passionate desire to sweep this hard Frenchman up into the thunder of the drum seized him. Louder and louder rolled the Advance. Who could resist it now? The drummer boy smiled triumphantly as he saw the little man's sea boot lift and fall . . . lift and fall as the beat broke into his heart.

The time was almost come. The corporal caught his eye – gave the ghost of a nod. He was the next to go.

But the drummer boy was sixty miles away. His regiments were marching to capture the sun. As in a dream he saw the cunning corporal seem to move without rising . . . as if the door itself was shifting towards his outstretched hand.

Suddenly everything stopped; the drum, the corporal and even the wizened potboy. A horrible thing had happened. The apple-cheeked man had stood up. He was staring at Corporal Finch. 'Was you going somewhere, friend?'

He spoke with a Wiltshire accent; but otherwise his tongue was all too plain. He was English; and likewise were all the rest! Grim, silent, betraying nothing, they'd listened in on every damning word; and, to the gaunt corporal's alarm, had understood each item of his abuse. He was still crouching, knees bent. Shock had deprived him of movement.

'Was you going somewhere, friend?' repeated the Wiltshire man, legs apart and fists ominously clenched.

The corporal stood upright. He drew in his breath then limped rapidly forward holding out a hand to be shook.

'Finch,' he said. 'By the grace of God a corporal and surviving. Thank the Lord you're on our side! It's a real honour, sir, to meet you 'ere! And – and if we offended, put it down to privation and the 'orrors of war! Drunk deep of death and danger, sir. Exposed our very 'earts to the battle's teeth. Gnawed us. Now you see us, tattered 'eroes, stripped of all but our lives and that precious flicker of la moor for our dear 'ome.'

The little man stared at the lofty corporal. He was taken

38

aback. Not being a military man himself, he'd met with nothing quite like Finch before. He opened his mouth – but the corporal was too quick for him. 'Parley not a word, sir! We ain't begging for pity! Though we was scattered like chaff before our enemies, our spirits ain't broke. Though they smote us with cruel steel, we live to fight another jewer. Take us 'ome and England'll bless you for it!'

The little man shook his head in wonderment – not knowing whether to laugh or pursue his first intention which had been to beat the corporal's brains out.

'How many are you?'

'Six, all told.'

'Money to pay?'

'We 'ave some few remembrances of the glorious mort,' said Finch cautiously.

'Three pound apiece and I'll take you,' said the Wiltshire man with a business-like air.

The corporal nodded; but Charlie Samson, still shaking under the humiliation of this last defeat, looked suddenly distressed. *His* only remembrance of the dead was a haunting dream and a lying letter. Not enough for his passage.

The Wiltshire man observed him. He smiled harshly. 'And I'll take your drummer boy as ballast.' Then he turned away – as if the brightness of the drummer boy's smile hurt his eyes.

Mister Shaw looked briefly mournful. He would have paid the drummer boy's passage, gladly . . . if he'd been given the chance.

The Wiltshire man's name was Isaac Gulliver. He dealt in brandy, tobacco and tea. He was a very prosperous smuggler on the Christchurch–Cherbourg run. But the evil weather of the past days had driven him so far off course that he'd run for shelter to this God-forsaken place.

Charlie knew of him. In the inns of Dorset and Hampshire, Gulliver was a household name. He sighed ruefully at this strange reminder of the home he'd left for better things.

But now they were to go. The tide would soon be on the turn and Isaac Gulliver and his dozen men had had their bellyful of fair France. They clumped out into the night – and the ancient potboy scuttled rapidly among the tumbled stools and benches as if to repair his web.

The longboat was already partly afloat. Beside it crouched Parsons, Mushoo and Edwards. They saw the oncoming army. Panic seized them. They turned to fly. Then the corporal waved and shouted: 'Joined forces! Fellow countrymen! Forchun's smiled at last!'

Two journeys were needed to bear the company out to the anchored vessel. Charlie Samson was of the second. Confused thoughts of the abandoned hillside filled him as he climbed into the longboat's stern and crouched on his drum. Then he felt in his pocket for the letter.

As he did so, he became aware of a figure standing just beyond the corner of his eye. Though it was dark, he knew this figure to be in scarlet; and he knew it was a figure he'd seen before – in the rain.

A leaden fear that the ghost was not to be left behind oppressed him. He turned. The figure did not vanish. It stood there, staring at him . . .

5

HE was not a ghost. Or if he was, he was a public one. Everyone saw him ... but got no pleasure from the sight. He looked more haunted than haunting; his face was unnaturally white and thin, his eyes were sunk and his condition worse than that of the survivors. Yet he had the price of his passage, and Isaac Gulliver – though even he shuddered – bade him climb aboard.

He crouched down beside Charlie and stared across the dark sea. He was trembling. He could not stop it. It was as if there was a chill within him that no mortal warmth could ease.

Charlie peered at his regimentals. He was a private soldier. With a sharp uneasiness, he saw he was of the Twenty-second Foot.

'Did you – did you ever know a James Digby?' Charlie asked.

No answer. The strange soldier seemed sunk too deep in his limitless despair.

Presently the fishing vessel loomed up above them. It was called the *Dove*. From its prow hung a monstrous carving of the bird of peace that had once carried an olive branch; but rough weather and the contemptuous sea had broken it off and left what seemed to be a beakful of savage teeth. It grinned across the longboat as if it knew a wicked secret.

'My name's Charlie,' said the drummer boy as they climbed aboard the *Dove*. 'Charlie Samson of the Twenty-eighth.' He held out his hand to be shook.

The strange soldier stared at him dully. Then a flicker came into his eyes. He struggled to smile, took the drummer boy's hand briefly in his own icy fingers. 'Maddox,' he muttered. 'Name of Maddox.'

'Up anchor, friends!' Isaac Gulliver had begun to give orders. His voice was hard as iron – but it was always 'friends'. Friends sweated on the anchor; friends loosed the foresail; friends belayed. Never was there such an affectionate ship as the *Dove*. Nonetheless, it made the survivors ponder on how Mr Gulliver might have dealt with an enemy.

Corporal Finch and his band moved from place to place about the deck, anxious to be in no one's way. From time to time they passed in the light of the mainmast lantern . . . rapid, uneasy, but above all, friendly.

The night winds began to blow across the deck and the foresail bloomed out like a dropsy. The dark waters coiled away and soon the *Dove* was clear of the little bay.

'Nor' by nor' west!' called Isaac Gulliver to the helmsman. 'Bring her over, friend!'

The *Dove* swung, briefly lost the wind, then caught it again. The sea tilted and the mainmast drew a line that cancelled half the stars.

'Me arm! Me arm! Oh God, it's smashed again!'

Unlucky Edwards, gaping at the sail, had been taken unawares. The leaning deck had shrugged him clean across its length like a bundle of old red rag. He lay against the side, moaning with despair. His arm – for pity's sake, take it off! No man had a right to be attached to such a wicked pain!

'Fetch him into the light,' ordered Mister Shaw. 'Gently with him!'

Mushoo and Parsons carried him to the main mast and laid him in the light of the mainmast lantern. Mr Gulliver and his friends looked on with interest.

But it seemed there was to be no amputation. Fat Mister Shaw, dainty as a mouse, unbound the injured limb and deftly corrected the damage before Edwards had a chance to shriek.

As he worked, the only sound to be heard was the wind sighing in the rigging. Mister Shaw was a craftsman to be watched. He had that skill in his trade there was no mistaking.

In his curious way the fat man was something of a genius. Charlie stared, fascinated by this oddness in nature.

Mister Shaw glanced at him, smiled wryly and murmured, 'Talent ain't particular where it nests, my dear.'

But most taken of all was Corporal Finch who brooded over the proceedings with awe. In the yellow lantern light his face might have been carved out of old pitted stone – with something hot within that gently steamed. He'd left his mouth ajar, displaying teeth like a street of failed tenements with doorways black as sin.

Mister Shaw sniffed and looked up. He frowned thoughtfully; then offered to fit the corporal with a set of teeth for fifteen pound. First class.

The corporal drew back. He looked affronted. That his appearance was susceptible of improvement had never struck him.

'Fresh French teeth,' urged Mister Shaw, finishing with Edwards and fumbling in one of his little leather bags.

He took out a forked incisor that had but lately filled in a young man's smile. He held it up, turning it this way and that. Charlie Samson shivered; but Corporal Finch was captivated.

'D'you see?' tempted Mister Shaw. 'Curved and hollowed the better to accommodate the French tongue?'

Mister Shaw had touched on the corporal's weakness. He sighed and began to fumble in his bottomless pockets. Watches, snuff boxes, gilt buttons and rings came up and glinted in the lantern light. Corporal Finch had enough remembrances of the glorious dead to last him to the grave and out the other side. He handled them shrewdly and concluded he could just afford a mouth of best French teeth, set, as the surgeon assured him, in untarnishable pewter.

One by one he put his treasures back till he came upon a battered silver watch that would never mark any hour beyond its owner's death. He squinted at an inscription upon its reverse. He peered round. He beamed, and beckoned with a long, crooked arm. He wanted the stranger – Maddox. The haunted

43

man came out of the shadows to the edge of the lantern light.

'This 'ere trifle,' said the corporal, holding out the silver watch. 'Seems it's from someone from the Twenty-second. Your lot, eh? Well – well! Take it to remind you! Say no more! Save your mercies to cool your consommy. Souvenir of the gurr.'

He gave the watch to Maddox and brushed aside his thanks. Corporal Finch was not an unkind man. He was as capable of sudden generosity as any man alive. That he was also capable of sudden villainy was only a mark of his general aptitude for staying alive.

Maddox drifted back to the side of the ship. From time to time he looked towards the survivors – as if to reassure himself that they were still there; but he made no effort to join them. It was an odd thing about him. Though he avoided company, he could not abide to be far from it.

Charlie watched him with pity. What had he seen on the hillside that had so ravaged him? A deep sympathy filled the drummer boy as he sensed in haunted Maddox an image of himself.

Maddox was staring at the watch. Charlie moved nearer, but Maddox was too absorbed to notice. The masthead lantern swung and stretched its light across the deck. Instinctively Maddox shrank from it; but not before Charlie had seen the look upon his face. He was staring at the watch as if he was terrified.

Impulsively Charlie spoke. 'Was it – was it off a friend?'

Maddox looked up. Glared frantically at the drummer boy. 'No! No!' He pressed himself backwards.

'Then . . . was it a – a brother?'

The haunted man's terror grew extreme. Much moved, Charlie took another pace. Suddenly Maddox flung up a hand as if to ward off the drummer boy. Then he turned and with a violent effort mounted the rail and leaped out into the night!

Amazed, Charlie saw his coat tails fly out like broken wings.

For an instant he vanished; then came the wild kiss as he struck the sea and made a silver flower in it.

'Maddox!' shrieked Charlie Samson. He struggled free of his drum and rushed to the side. 'Maddox!'

But Maddox was gone. Confusion broke out on the deck. Lanterns swung – voices shouted. 'Charlie! Come back! You're mad –'

The drummer boy had followed after the suicide. A dark arm had come up out of the sea and seemed to beckon . . .

He struck the water some six or eight yards after where Maddox had vanished and at once he was engulfed in a freezing, salty darkness. It swallowed up his mouth and nose and eyes, and seemed to penetrate into the inmost chamber of his head. But worst of all was the dreadful clammy embrace of his clothes. He could scarcely move against it.

A violent terror seized him. He was being dragged down. The little waves were on a level with his eyes, and growing taller. Like regiments they came at him, casting their plumes and freezing scarves across his head. Despairingly he tried to beat them back; but how could one drummer boy hold off an army?

He twisted his head further and further back; then queerly remembered his mother washing his hair in a great copper basin by the fire.

So began his short life to pass in review before him; for he was beginning to drown. 'Don't struggle, Charlie . . . don't struggle . . .' her voice sang in his ears. Piteously he looked up, half expecting her face.

But instead something vast and round flew out of the sky and struck the sea with a loud commotion! He reached towards it, wearily obeying urgent voices that seemed to be a thousand miles away. 'Hold it, Charlie . . . don't struggle . . . hold it!'

It perched on the water, turning over and over like a fallen moon. It was his drum.

He touched it. His fingers gripped the gilded cording that caged the barrel. It tried to dance away, then bobbed back and

45

gently nudged the drummer boy's cheek – as if it was fond of him. Now the boy caught it in a full embrace; and the drum sustained him.

The *Dove* had turned. Lanterns glimmered all about her. Ropes were over her side and friends of Mr Gulliver were clinging to them, ready to take the drummer boy up out of the sea. Above them clustered faces the drummer boy had never thought to see again.

He was almost within the sailors' grasp when abruptly there broke out of the sea beside him a weird and uncanny sight. Maddox rose gleaming from the water like he was carved from it. The sea streamed out of his cropped hair and vanished over his white face in a terrified grin. The last of the air in his lungs had drawn him up to take its departure.

Charlie reached out and grasped the shining coat. Some feeble struggles and jerkings as if of protest rewarded him. But they were not strong enough to break free; Maddox continued to grin frozenly into his eyes while twitching to be free. Then the sailors caught hold and heaved man, boy and drum on to the deck.

For a long while nothing stood between Maddox and death but the strength of Mister Shaw. He fought a great battle. Ceaselessly he chafed and rubbed and worried at the dying man, sometimes even seeming to blow on the fragile flicker of life within him till at last it began to glow. Maddox stirred and moaned; whereupon the fat man drew breath and went to work again till the sweat poured off him in a torrent. At last he stopped. Maddox's chest rose and fell of its own accord. Then Mister Shaw went back to a more profitable task. He was measuring Corporal Finch's rubbish heap of a mouth for fresh French teeth.

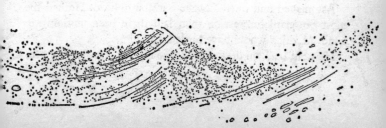

But Charlie Samson, his clothes somewhat shrunk in drying, stalked the windy deck in a mood of tolerance mixed with grandeur – and wearing a tricorne hat given him by an admirer.

Next day the sun shone, but it was as nothing to the shining of the drummer boy. He marched in everyone's heart. He was a hero, and even Isaac Gulliver smiled as he passed . . .

Then the sun went down and the *Dove* passed on through the night – a little, coursing lamplit world. The survivors, huddled about the deck, dozed and dreamed of easy days on profits to be got from their remembrances. But beyond this, they refused to dream. They'd survived the fury of the French; surely they'd scrape through the indifference of the English? They mumbled and started – then sank back into snores.

Mister Shaw dreamed of teeth; of Charlie Samson taking him to Bruton Street, and of a rich household lacking for nothing save gnashers. 'Fifty pound . . .' he breathed; then rolled over and buzzed like a compost heap.

The drummer boy himself still walked the deck. The event that had made him a hero had already begun to seem like a dream. Was there really a man called Maddox who'd jumped into the sea? He went down to the tiny cabin that Isaac Gulliver had given up to the sick man. Mr Gulliver's friends, on eternal watch, nodded and smiled as he passed.

Yes – there was such a man. He lay in the narrow bunk with his exhausted eyes turned on the door as if in constant expectation.

Charlie beamed at him – and a great feeling of affection welled up in him. But Maddox did not seem to return it. Though he thanked Charlie three or four times, all the while he seemed to be trying to escape him. At last he could contain himself no longer. 'Why do you meddle with me? Leave me alone – for God's sake!'

Astonished and hurt, Charlie Samson obliged. He had the most powerful impression that, had there been anything to hand, Maddox would have hurled it at him.

He went back on deck to compose himself. He stepped over

Mister Shaw who woke and mumbled, 'Won't be long, my dear. And then it's Bruton Street, eh? Must break the sad news to the lady. The letter . . .' Then he went back to sleep again and his fat face creased in a greedy smile.

Charlie moved to the side of the ship, his thoughts still with ungrateful Maddox. He stared outward. The night was clear. The stars and a cutlass moon flickered on the moving water where they were multiplied ten thousand times among the waves. They jiggled up and down in endless lines like the polished tops of muskets, shouldered high. Presently a sad smile came over the drummer boy's face.

Suddenly someone was standing by him! Just beyond the corner of his eye: a figure in scarlet . . . He turned, but it was gone. Uneasily, he felt in his pocket for the letter. The paper was torn and white. The sea had washed it clean.

Again he sensed the figure to be close. It was behind him – in the quiet sea. Its head was broken and bloody . . . and it whispered in the drummer boy's ear: 'They will not let me in . . . your scarlet men. I am an outcast . . .'

With a groan, Charlie turned about. Nothing but the darkly glittering waters.

'My letter –'

'It's gone,' whispered the boy.

'But you remember it . . . every word. The death in battle of James Digby . . .'

'No! No!'

He turned and twisted to catch a sight of the figure in scarlet; but always it was beyond the corner of his eye . . . now beside him, now behind him, now in the hollow of his drum.

'Whose heart will have me unless you unlock it, Charlie? You must – you must! Tell my love I died bravely; and give me peace, my friend.'

In anguish the boy answered, 'If I do – if I do, will you give *me* peace?'

'Oh yes . . . *I* will give you peace, my friend . . .'

6

THE survivors' hopes had been raised better than their dreams. They had been offered congenial employment. Isaac Gulliver's affairs had reached such prosperity that they needed to expand – or they would burst.

He had his eye on a natural premises near Burley in the New Forest for a store from which to distribute his goods farther east and north than ever before.

Though he knew nothing of military matters, shrewd observation of Corporal Finch and his band had convinced him that Nature herself had created them to be storesmen. They had the very air of having been not so much born as indented for.

The corporal was very happy, and it brought out the gaunt humanity in him. Kindly he asked his companions whether any of them had 'a little woman' or 'a clutch of nippers' waiting on his return. He'd stand between no man and his responsibilities. But it seemed nothing was waiting for them that they'd not gladly left behind. Parsons, Edwards and Mushoo pledged allegiance; Charlie Samson, however, shook his head.

''Ome, lad? Going 'ome?'

'No . . .' He frowned deeply. He'd not shaken the dust of Lyndhurst from his feet to have it blow straight back in his face. 'A – a promise. I'm going to London . . . to Bruton Street, you know . . .'

Mister Shaw pricked up his ears. So the drummer boy was really going to unlock the golden door? He drew close and smiled hopefully.

Maddox. What of Maddox? The survivors glanced at one another. No one wanted him. The odour of calamity hung too heavy about him. Then once again humanity got the better of the corporal. He shrugged his shoulders and suggested that a life in the woods might raise even his doused spirits to a natural height. Let him stay . . .

Soon after midnight on May twenty-five, the *Dove* came in to nest. A little cove between Christchurch and Poole where even the sea came in on tiptoe so as not to wake the Revenue Men.

By half after two the *Dove* had laid its private egg upon the sand – a sinful monument of stacked up casks of brandy and wine. The vessel nodded peacefully under the moon, turning this way and that. Presently, the grin on her ragged beak seemed to broaden. The pale shore was empty; her egg was gone.

Three bulbous waggons were lumbering north. Their wheels were bandaged, their harness muffled. Across open country and down discreet lanes they rumbled, through the remainder of the night and into the golden striped morning. Still they continued, past noon and into the late afternoon. Then the Forest reached out to welcome them – as if it had been waiting.

Somewhat tipsily they rolled into the cathedral of trees, like three huge hooded friars creeping to Vespers. Down winding aisles they moved, past chapels of oak and crypts of hawthorn and holly, all stained with the blood of the setting sun.

Isaac Gulliver's men walked ahead, with cautious pace and wary eyes. At the rear stalked the survivors – all save Edwards whose injury kept him within a waggon. Corporal Finch peered round at the huge dim forest with a mixture of arrogance and awe. He was aware of conflict: Nature's nature and his own. But he was not to be defeated. All things yielded to education . . . and he, Corporal Finch, was ready, willing and able to learn a bit about trees. A look of confidence came over his bird-like face, and he walked with a respectful swagger.

But Charlie Samson saw the forest more domestically. He

51

was disagreeably near his home ... and recalled again the defiance with which he'd left it.

He walked in dread of coming upon his father – even though Lyndhurst was all of eight miles off. Mr Samson was a great forest lover – in every sense of the word; he was also a Royalist. His eldest born he'd called 'Rufus', on account of his having been conceived at King's Gutter where the gypsies knew the unlucky king had perished. ('For ain't there a stream hard by, wrapped in alders, that runs red each year on the day he died?')

His second had been conceived near Furzey and called 'John' after a prince who'd been perforated with arrows on the very spot.

Charlie himself had been conceived at King's Hat where Mr Samson was entirely persuaded the Martyr King had halted for a prayer. After which he and Mrs Samson walked but rarely in the woods, preferring to keep to their inn which was called The Doe's Rest.

Charlie had visited King's Hat. A pretty spot in bluebell time. He wondered what the lovers had been thinking of, or whether any forest phantom had passed them by to have bequeathed him so haunted a turn of mind.

At last the waggons halted. Mr Gulliver's new premises had been reached; three forest huts the gypsies had once inhabited – and left for better things.

Ragged bushes accosted them, tapped on their roofs and plucked at their broken doorways as if inquisitive to see if they were alive.

Somewhat discouraged, the survivors squinted at their new home. Then Corporal Finch rubbed his hands together and stalked into the middle hut. From darkest nowhere he found an ancient chair, sat on it, and, with his claw-like hands engulfing his knees, peered out at the forest world; a seedy King of the Wood upon his battered throne.

The waggons were being unloaded. Cask after cask beaded

53

out of one concealment and, on sweating shoulders, vanished into another at the back of the huts. Isaac Gulliver, legs apart and hands at his belt, watched the passage of the unholy rosary. His lips moved as he told it off. At last he turned to his new quartermaster.

'They're counted, friend. Every last one. So just you remember, it's not King George you're answerable to, but Isaac Gulliver.' He scowled menacingly, then went on to promise the corporal that all his indentings and invoicings and stock-taking would be most carefully overlooked by a certain Mr Walsh of Burley ...

'We don't foul our own nest,' interrupted the corporal, looking more bird-like than ever among the tangled foliage that nudged his hut. 'And this 'ere place, among these 'ere 'arbers, is our private nest.'

Isaac Gulliver sighed. He and Corporal Finch had reached that point beyond which no profit was possible without a measure of trust. It wasn't a point the smuggler cared for. Always he tried to avoid it, with threats and a whole tribe of Mr Walshes. But sooner or later, in all his dealings, there it was – the little quicksand on the way to success. Another's word ...

Corporal Finch was holding out his hand to be shaken. Isaac Gulliver took it and stared very intently into his quarter-master's eyes, as if he was considering taking a lease on them. The corporal beamed.

Now the light was almost gone and the waggons were ready to depart. The survivors gathered in the mouths of the huts to watch them on their way. Once more like three huge hooded friars they rolled. Their devotions ended, they carried little lanterns high, as if to light them to their nightly cells. For a while these lanterns winked among the trees, till, one by once, the darkness pricked them out.

'Bonn wee,' murmured Corporal Finch and settled himself down in his hut. The others poked and ferreted about discon-solately for a while, then they too found nesting places for the night.

'Corp!' came Parsons' voice softly from a shadow. No reply. Leading the way in everything, Corporal Finch was already asleep.

Presently the quartermaster's store began to buzz and hum to a consort of snores. Near at hand an owl – too easily astonished – screeched three or four times; then seemed satisfied to let the hours take their softly rustling course.

Trees, bushes and the very huts themselves deepened and hedged their outlines till they took on the aspect of dreams and became whatever the forest willed. Then, little by little, the darkness died and there stood in its place the spectral daylight of the moon. The endless forest rustling stopped. The air was still and the trees seemed to be standing in a silver silence for the ceremony of the night. The empty bodies of the survivors rose and fell as their leashed spirits wandered abroad . . . in ale houses, pawn shops and ladies' chambers . . .

But the drummer boy was awake. He was staring at a particular part of the forest. A hole in the silver; a ragged black patch into which a figure had seemed to vanish – out of the corner of his eye. His heart beat fiercely.

'W – was it you, James Digby?'

He began to creep towards where it had gone – when he sensed the figure to be behind him. If he turned he knew it would vanish. Yet he had to turn. Maddox was standing and glaring at him!

'What – what is it?'

The haunted man's face shone in the moonlight. It was glazed with tears.

'What is it?'

'I – I beg you . . . don't go to Bruton Street. Don't go there! Don't – don't . . .'

'But – why not?'

'Don't go!' The words came out like musket fire: sharp, desperate.

7

THE morning was golden again. Sunlight flickered down through the forest like a storm of butterflies, feeding on leaves, branches and, briefly, on Corporal Finch's beaked nose.

The corporal was inquiring when he might expect his teeth. The prospect of fine French gnashers had made him so dissatisfied with the state of his mouth that he'd paid Mister Shaw five pounds in advance.

'Three – four weeks, Finch.'

The corporal sighed. Now it was his turn to be on the wrong end of trust. He stared unhappily at the fat, shifty surgeon, all tabby in the sun. Then he brightened at the sight of the drummer boy beside him. Honesty shone from the warrior lad like a beacon. The corporal shook him by the hand, wished him well and slipped in a hope that he'd not forget his companion de la gurr waiting toothless in the wood.

'And may the bonn Dew bring you back safe and soon!' he called out as the surgeon and the drummer boy set off for Ringwood and the London coach. Then he went back to his hut.

Mushoo alone watched after them. The Frenchman's eyes were bright with a problem. Suddenly he could endure the uncertainty no longer. He hastened after and caught up with Mister Shaw. The surgeon turned in surprise.

'Zee teet'!' panted Mushoo. 'French teet' is better, yes?' He grinned, as if to show off these natural advantages. Mister Shaw grinned back at him . . . and Mushoo nodded. Then, his English exhausted, he trotted back, wrapped in his quaint rags of national pride.

Strangely moved, Charlie saw that the Frenchman's head

was held somewhat higher and his step had become more springy on the alien ground.

They reached Ringwood two hours before the London coach was to set off, so the surgeon and the drummer boy went to a barber's to have the filth and bristle of their journey from the hillside scraped away. Mister Shaw, rouged, repaired and smelling like a flower, came out into the sun and preened himself. Then out came Charlie Samson, and the surgeon smiled painfully to see, in place of the battle-haunted, tattered drummer boy on whom his affections were helplessly pinned, the fresh and shining golden lad. He felt himself to be suddenly crumpled and blowsy.

They travelled by way of Salisbury on the coach's roof. Mister Shaw advanced Charlie the money – on account of expectations from Bruton Street. Even sad news, the surgeon said knowledgeably, must be rewarded; while the prospect of getting his fat foot inside General Lawrence's house made him sweat with anticipation.

Nothing short of a convulsion in nature would have separated him from the drummer boy. Beside Mister Shaw limpets and leeches were off-hand in their attachments.

The day continued fair and the coach rattled briskly along the striped roads. At every jolt, Charlie's drum (from which he was not to be parted) boomed anxiously, and the coachman's ribboned pigtail danced against his back like a startled black moth.

Fellow passengers, whatever they might have thought of painted Mister Shaw, observed the dummer boy with pleasure. In his heroic person he answered many an idea and dream.

Little by little, under the influence of the splendour of the day, Charlie Samson's troubles abated. He'd not seen his ghost since aboard the *Dove*; and even the wild words of Maddox lost their sharp terror and became no more than the mutterings of a man distracted with grief.

'Don't go to Bruton Street . . .' Charlie frowned and shook

his head. What could there be in Bruton Street to shake a survivor from the blazing hillside? He had stalked drumming through the worst men could do. He had walked with a ghost and kept his own soul secure. He smiled haughtily as he recalled these things. What darker terrors could there be to come?

Suddenly he sensed there was a newcomer on the coach. He turned to look behind him. There was no one. His face grew pale. His heart sank. It had been the ghost. Even in bold sunshine in a Hampshire lane.

This was bad. He had not escaped the phantom. Somewhere in the invisible air it was grinning at him. He knew it.

'Tell her I died bravely . . .'

'I'll tell her you died –' answered the frightened drummer boy. 'No more than that!'

Mister Shaw glanced at him curiously; but held his peace. After a moment the surgeon returned to his study of the passing world; but his expression had lost a little of its contentment . . .

At about ten o'clock in the morning of May twenty-nine, they passed the apple stall at Hyde Park Corner. Already the air stank rich and heavy and the sun seemed to be seen through dusty glass. It was as if all the busy Town was shut up in a cabinet that no one had opened for years.

They took rooms at the White Horse Cellar in Piccadilly, and once more the drummer boy was beholden to the fat surgeon.

'An investment, my dear,' said Mister Shaw airily. 'Think nothing of it. The dividend will come from Bruton Street. Just introduce me and talent will do the rest.'

Awkwardly Charlie glanced at him. The surgeon, despite his paint and perfume, was a flabby, wretched sight. Even in the careless streets, Mister Shaw received contemptuous looks. But he rode them like a cork and bounced along beside the drummer boy who hurried, partly to have done with his strange task and partly in the forlorn hope of outpacing Mister Shaw.

They were in Old Bond Street which had come out in a rash of spotted muslins as London ladies took the air. Faces turned and stared after Charlie Samson. Helplessly hearts quickened and wistful smiles sweetened painted lips as the drummer boy passed haughtily by.

Then, quite suddenly, these hearts contracted. The drummer boy had halted. His face had gone as pale as death. He trembled –

'It's nothing!' panted Mister Shaw anxiously. 'Only a coincidence, my dear!'

The boy was on a corner, staring up at the facing wall. It was *Maddox* Street.

'Don't go – don't go!' Maddox's words sighed and roared through his head like a dark wind foretelling calamity.

'We've come too far. The other side . . .' Mister Shaw was pulling at him. Passers-by stared . . .

Then an elderly gentleman, unable to resist temptation, rapped neatly on Charlie's drum as he strolled, humming by. The drummer boy started and caught sight of a sternish face with a childish twinkle.

Indignantly Charlie frowned; and his fears sank. He suffered Mister Shaw to lead him back across the street. At last they came to Bruton Street.

Two brisk officers were turning out of it. They saw the drummer boy. Gallantly they saluted him . . . and Charlie Samson, with a rush of his old innocence, raised a drumstick in reply.

'General Lawrence's house?' called Mister Shaw after them. They stopped. 'Corner of the Square. Can't miss it.' They laughed. 'His colours are over the door!' Then they sauntered on.

The General. Charlie had seen him once, stalking the lines on his chestnut horse. A glittering and imposing sight, even from afar. Momentarily he was awed at the prospect of meeting with him; then Mister Shaw gripped his arm. They had reached the house.

The General's colours? Over his door was a lozenge of black. It was a hatchment. The knocker was muffled in crepe; and upon the step stood a lean man in cloth as black as night. He was a mute. The General's house was in mourning. His colours were the colours of death.

8

'Son-in-law,' said the mute who did not live up to his name, preferring to take a more lively interest in his deathlihood, so to speak. 'Major Fitzwarren, God rest him. Passed away in battle. Leaves a widow and child.'

'May we go in?' asked Mister Shaw. The mute gazed disparagingly at the curious pair. 'Friends of the family?'

'Comrades in arms,' said Mister Shaw. 'We were there when he fell.'

'Ah, but now you're here,' said the mute shrewdly.

'Letter. The lad has a letter for Miss Sophia Lawrence.'

The mute frowned. He wasn't sure . . . didn't know . . . but he'd inquire. He raised his black-mittened hand out of which his fingers poked like five grimy worms and buried them in the crepe round the knocker. 'No remains to be viewed, you understand,' he said warningly. 'Grave on the field with 'is comrades. Only a few personal items laid out. Minichers and 'air brushes, like. And of course 'is widow . . .' He knocked on the door and a footman answered. 'Two more,' said the mute.

The footman peered at the fat, seedy surgeon and the nervous drummer boy. 'I'll convey your condolences,' he said coolly.

Once again Mister Shaw confided: 'Letter. The lad has a letter from the battlefield . . . for Miss Sophia.'

The effect was extraordinary. The footman seemed to back away. An uneasy, almost frightened look came into his eyes. He glanced briefly upward, then muttered, 'You'd best come in, then.'

As they passed over the threshold, the mute drifted out his hand and Mister Shaw slapped a shilling in it like a poultice.

Then the house's shadow cut off the sunshine as if with an axe and the door was shut behind them.

Candles burned in sconces round the hall and the air was heavy with a curiously sweetish smell.

'You'd best see the General first,' said the footman, and again glanced towards the top of the house. It seemed to the frightened drummer boy that, far more than grief, it was the presence of Sophia Lawrence that brooded over the house like an ominous cloud . . .

Mirrors. There were a great many mirrors in the hall and on the stairway; and on each carved and inlaid frame was perched a fledgling of crepe. As they mounted the stairs towards the General's drawing-room, Charlie saw Mister Shaw's eager face appear in glass after glass like a row of portraits, each more unflattering than the last.

Then suddenly the drawing-room door burst open. The footman had scarcely time to stand aside for a gentleman in grey who came rapidly out and hastened down the stairs. He brushed against the drummer boy, smiled thinly, and was gone.

'Papa! Papa!' came a woman's voice from the room. It was distressed, alarmed.

Mister Shaw waddled ahead. 'Surgeon,' he cried to the footman. 'I'm a surgeon!'

'Papa!' The widow, pale as a lily in her weeds, was kneeling beside her huge father who was collapsed in a chair. Like a fallen conflagration he slumped there, blazing in his uniform, and wearing a narrow armband of black. His powerful face was flushed to the colour of his coat. Charlie feared a seizure.

Mister Shaw was at his side. God knew how the fat man had moved so quick, for the room was immense. He was feeling the General's wrist, touching the side of his massive head. 'I'm a surgeon, ma'am,' he murmured to the widow. Then he frowned and stood back. 'I – I think he will recover shortly,' he said. 'Perhaps a glass of brandy . . .?'

General Lawrence breathed deeply, and with Mister Shaw's

anxious and humble assistance, stood upright. His hand was clutching at his heart. He turned to the widow, but she'd gone back to her chair at the table on which her dead husband's 'personal items' were laid out. She glanced curiously at the drummer boy who stood in the doorway.

'They've come –' began the footman apologetically, when she waved him away with abrupt peevishness.

The General had managed to achieve the mantelpiece. He rested against it and gazed at his face in a large gilt mirror that was partly entombed in crepe.

'It's nothing . . . nothing,' he muttered, seeming to draw comfort from his soldierly reflection. Presently he turned to face the room. He bowed his head. 'You too . . . you too. Have you come to blame me?' He peered under his thick brows from the surgeon to the tattered, upright drummer boy. Then catching sight of himself in the polished brass of the drum, he drew himself up. 'Gentlemen, you must excuse me. I have had a great shock . . . great shock.'

Suddenly from behind the widow's chair, a small object in black appeared. It was a child – a boy of about four.

'They're going to hang Grandpapa!' he chanted shrilly. 'And chop off his head!'

Feebly the widow bade him hold his tongue; but the damage had been done. The General was down again in his chair, his head in his large, strong hands. 'The child tells the truth,' he whispered. 'But I blame no one. Least of all –' Here, he lifted his head and gazed at the widow who turned away sharply. 'Least of all your husband, my dear. Don't think I'm afraid to die. God knows I've still my pride.' He stared at Charlie's drum. 'Ten thousand men fell on that terrible morning. *Their* heads were high; *their* hearts were true. *They* showed me the way! No: I am not afraid. I would put a bullet through my brain gladly . . . but they say that's the coward's way.'

The General was up again. Whatever else, he was not a coward. He was not, under any circumstances, going to shoot himself. He was going to face the forces that were gathering to destroy him. He was going to face his court martial.

Though he himself blamed no one, many blamed him. The Duke blamed him; the Minister – who'd just left – blamed him; and soon, ten thousand widows would be blaming him.

Very well; he would submit. Oh God! The responsibility of high command! 'Would that I were a humble drummer boy with all the world in my drum!' He continued to stare absorbedly at the drum.

'Do you blame me, young man?' He observed the facings

on Charlie's uniform. 'You were there, weren't you? Do you lay it all on me? It matters to me . . . it does indeed. If you don't blame me, then perhaps my brave men will not either.'

Bewildered, the drummer boy shook his head. The vast calamity of the hillside had seemed more like an act of God than the fault of a single man. But what had the dead major to do with it?

'Nor would I have you blame my poor son-in-law.'

'For God's sake, Papa!' interrupted the widow. 'He's dead – he's dead! Spare his child –'

'My dear,' said the General kindly, 'I was only going to explain to the – er – gentlemen that I hold nothing against him now. I forgive him.' He turned back to Mister Shaw and Charlie. 'You see, my son-in-law was – was unfortunate. Ill-placed. The wrong man in the wrong situation. Not his fault, d'you see?' And before the dead man's widow could halt him, the General explained.

On that brilliant morning the Duke had been so eager to advance. All that stood in his way was the wood – the pretty little wood. The General had foreseen the Duke's eagerness and dispatched his aide, Major Fitzwarren, to make sure it was clear.

'Then, as I'd foreseen, the Duke rides up. 'All clear, Lawrence, eh? Ready to advance? Capture the sun, ha-ha!' So I send for Fitzwarren. 'The wood, sir. Have you searched?' He looks me in the eye – and nods. Yes. He nodded. A terrible nod, that. And I *knew* he'd not gone! I'd seen him, with my own eyes, skulking behind a company of grenadiers. But – but what could I do? There was the Duke . . . and there was my son-in-law. Almost my flesh and blood. Trust. I had to show trust, you understand. There comes a time, eh? Yet I don't blame him. Weak . . . weak . . . But he paid his debt. Paid it in full, eh? And now – now his father-in-law must pay all over again. Why, might you ask? Revenge? No. Justice? No. Finding a scapegoat? No. The General is blamed because no one saw him give the order to search the wood. And the only man who could have supported him and confirmed that such an order was given, lies gloriously dead on that hillside. But for his widow's and son's sake, I will not blame him. Pride, gentlemen. I have my pride. They shall not break it.'

By dint of quick, sustaining glances from mirror to polished drum, the General had got command over himself. Smiling, he glanced from the surgeon to the drummer boy. 'I don't suppose, gentlemen, that either of *you* chanced to be on hand when I gave that order? Please don't feel obliged to answer! Indeed, I'm sorry I asked! Ashamed! Yes, I'm ashamed I mentioned it! What must you think of me?' He'd fixed his pale, fierce eyes on the drummer boy. 'You must think your general is frightened . . . is trying to save his skin. But, believe me, it is not for my own sake that I ask. It is for –' His voice had grown low – and the drummer boy was suddenly chilled to the bone. The General had glanced upward, to somewhere at the top of the house; and into his eyes had come an uneasy, almost frightened look.

'It is for *her*; for my daughter Sophia . . . She – she is not very strong. The shock of my fall would undoubtedly kill her. Her death would be on my head. So – so I try to keep it from her. She must not know. All must be kept quiet till –'

The General stopped. A black speck – a cinder – had darted out again from behind the widow's chair: the dead man's child. His mother reached out; too late. The child flew to the shining drum. He raised his fists and brought them down on the tight skin in an unholy tattoo.

The sound in the quiet house was enormous. It rolled and roared and thundered. It echoed from cellar to attic till the very bricks seemed to shake and shudder to the terrible sound of the military drum.

The child fled, appalled by what he'd done. Then the sound died away, and the General stared towards the open door. In the quietness there came the sound of a creak on the stair, then a sharp rustling . . .

She wore a dark red gown and a shawl of black taffeta that enfolded her like the wings of some huge dark bird. Sophia Lawrence . . .

She was bewilderingly beautiful. Never in his life before had the drummer boy seen anything so piercingly lovely. Her complexion was very pale, but her hair was black as pitch. It was a profound, passionate black such as certain rich colours assume under the moon. She leaned against the door post. 'What is it? I heard such a – a warlike noise.' She smiled. 'I thought all the King's men had come!'

'Nothing, my dear! Only your nephew. Nothing at all. Go back, now –'

'But our visitors, Papa. Are they from the – the battlefield? Surely this drummer boy has come from there. He's just as I dreamed –' She paused to draw breath, as if the effort of descending the stairs was still affecting her. She gazed at the drummer boy whose heart had begun to thunder like an echo of his drum. Her eyes widened. Two spots of red appeared on the crests of her cheeks. 'Why do you look so? What is it you see? Am I a ghost?'

The drummer boy was trembling visibly. He had seen a horrible thing. Round about Sophia, flickering like some malignant scarlet lightning, was the spectre of her dead lover! Now above her head, now at her side . . . plucking at her; and gibbering wildly at the drummer boy . . . Then it was gone.

'I – I –' began the boy.

'A message,' murmured Mister Shaw, observing Sophia intently. 'He has a letter for you.'

She looked to the painted fat man – then dropped her eyes. The red spots in her cheeks spread into a blush.

'From James? Is it from James?' Once more she was staring at Charlie. He could not escape her eyes. They seemed to burn.

'He's dead. I know it. I see it in your face. Oh my poor, poor friend!'

Miserably the drummer boy nodded

67

'Oh God!' groaned the General. 'Is there nothing but bad news that comes to this accursed house?'

'Dear Papa.' She smiled at him – and the General raised his head with a poignant dignity that seemed of more consequence than all his mirror-fed pride. 'When he chose a soldier's life he purchased a soldier's death. None of us lives for ever – save in each other's hearts.' Yet again she'd turned to the drummer boy; but the smile did not leave her lips.

'Better to go in a blaze than dwindle to a burnt-out cinder,' she said. 'For when all's said and done, it's the going that counts.'

She stopped. Her shawl rustled ceaselessly with the unequal rising and falling of her breast.

'My dear . . . my dear,' murmured her father. 'I cannot say how sorry I am.'

She shook her head. 'Perhaps he will tell me about – it; in my own parlour? I would like to hear . . . to know. With your permission, Papa . . . please?'

The General bowed his head; and fleetingly there crossed Sophia's face a look of triumph. She turned and swayed and rustled towards the stairs. Helplessly the drummer boy began to follow; when the General moved quickly to his side.

'Young man!' he muttered. 'Be gentle. Nothing harsh, violent, you understand? And above all, nothing about what I've said! Spare her as long as you can! Ah! if only you'd heard my order! *Then* we might have saved her! But it cannot be. No. I don't blame you . . . I blame no one . . .'

9

THE curious sweetish smell that pervaded the house seemed strongest in Sophia's parlour. It was a small, bright room papered with a design of trellises, leaves and purple flowers so bold and lifelike that the heavy perfume seemed to be coming from them.

But otherwise all was graceful and delicate and the drummer boy moved with extreme caution for fear of laying it waste. He settled his drum in the middle of the floor . . . and it looked like a tombstone in a nursery. He felt monstrously out of place.

There was a couch by the window from which the room's strange mistress might watch the sunlit square. But now she lay back, watching the drummer boy. Her gown overflowed and tumbled to the floor where it caught the sunlight and turned to blood.

'The letter.'

'It's gone. The – the sea took it.'

'The words. You remember them?'

Charlie Samson looked guiltily round the room. But nothing was by. They were alone. 'No. Not every one –'

'Liar!'

Who'd spoken? Not she? No. Her face was still – even calm.

'Tell me . . . how did he look?'

'I – I found him . . . with the letter in his hand. He was done for, you know . . . quite kippered . . .' The General's words dinned in his brain. He must be gentle. Nothing harsh. 'The moonlight made him all silver. He was very peaceful looking.'

'And the letter? Can you remember nothing of it?'

Again he glanced round the room; most particularly behind

him. 'He – he said he loved you . . . with all his heart and all his soul and all his might.'

She turned her face towards the window and Charlie saw that her thin fingers were gripping her taffeta shawl till the bones shone. He dreaded an outburst of injurious despair. But no such outburst came. Though outwardly she was frail, even desperately so, yet there seemed much strength within.

'The hillside. Tell me about it.' Her voice was so slow that Charlie moved closer to catch her words. 'What was it like there?'

The drummer boy frowned. 'As far as the eye could see, scarlet men were marching. The hillside was in bloom with them . . .'

As he talked, he began to live it again. In his mind's eye, the tall men smiled – and smiling, went to their deaths high up on the hill.

The pallid young woman on the couch was sitting upright. Her eyes shone and her black shawl rustled unendingly as her breath came quick. This rustling was a noticeable quality of hers. It always seemed to accompany her.

Otherwise, all infirmity seemed to have left her. She listened in brilliance, and the drummer boy sensed his own medicinal power. A feeling of ease and joy began to inspire him as he told of the terror and grandeur of the morning . . . and he watched Sophia blossom fierily against the paper trellises and leaves.

The sweetish perfume seemed to increase and the air grow thick with it. His mind began to tilt and his thoughts to slip and tumble, as if he'd had too much of Mr Samson's strong ale.

He came to tell of the night and his lonely rising among the windfall of dead . . . the misty banners and broken swords, the buttons that glinted like fallen stars. Then his drum, lying there . . .

Sophia glanced at it, gleaming in the middle of her delicate parlour. Charlie nodded. It was the same. The very drum on

70

which he'd tapped the Funeral Retreat for the fallen scarlet men.

He paused – for now he'd come to Corporal Finch and the survivors. Somehow it was they who seemed more dreamlike in the substance of his dream . . . even nightmarish. So he made no mention of them.

'The Retreat,' murmured Sophia unevenly. 'Please, will you play it now? I would like to hear . . . but softly, softly –'

By now Charlie Samson was quite overthrown by his own powers. In a state of exaltation he took up his drum and slung it from his shoulders. Then, with head held high and drumsticks lifting with splendid arrogance, he played the Funeral Retreat; but softly . . . softly . . .

As Sophia listened an intolerable agitation seemed to possess her. She rose from the couch and began to move about the room, as if she, like the soldiers, was but an obedient spirit of the drum.

For some seconds she stood behind the drummer boy. He trembled as he felt her breath brushing his cheek. He turned his head. Her face was on a level with his. Her eyes were blazing with tears. Gently she came nearer . . . and Charlie held his breath and kissed her eyes.

That his neck was at an odd angle, owing to the awkwardness of the drum between them, made him be brief. He blushed and begged her pardon. All in all, he'd taken quite a liberty with his general's daughter.

But she –? She smiled at him as if she'd have laughed. She shook her head. 'Oh my drummer boy! My drummer boy come home from the wars!'

At once, a feeling of triumphant relief swept over the boy.

'What is your name, drummer boy?'

'Samson. Charlie Samson –'

'Why, that's a hero's name!'

'I – I never chose it.'

'But you chose – that!' She touched the skin of his drum . . . and unaccountably Charlie shuddered.

She went back to the couch. Of a sudden, her energy seemed spent. The colour was gone from her cheeks and the fire from her eyes. She lay back. 'Will you come again, Charlie Samson? Please come again. Only now – now I must rest. I'm so tired . . .'

She reached out for a little gilt bell that stood on a table beside her. 'Sunlight becomes you, Charlie Samson. You shine in it . . . like gold. Will you grow old, drummer boy? Will you tarnish and wrinkle and bend and hobble by the wayside in the wake of your own soul? Or – or –' Her voice sank to a breathing whisper. The fire glinted briefly in her eyes. 'Or will you –'

She rang the bell and drowned her own words with it. But the drummer boy knew them. She had whispered, 'Or will you come with me?'

A servant answered the bell: a pretty girl in a cap and black gown out of which a petticoat kept dancing as if it was putting its tongue out at the world. She glanced at the drummer boy respectfully, then curtsied as her mistress bade her show him out.

On the stairs she paused. 'My name's Charity,' she said. 'What might yours be?'

Charlie frowned. Though her tone was as respectful as her manner, there was something at the back of it that reminded him disturbingly of all the Lyndhurst lasses who'd ever tossed their heads to his friendly winks.

'Samson,' he answered coldly. 'Charles Samson.'

'Glad to meet you, Charlie.' She glanced at the large, glimmering drum. 'It's brass, ain't it? Real brass? Well – well! Tell you what; there's a tinker up the road who'll give you a shilling for it!' Then she shook her head as if mightily puzzled over the ways of the warrior world. The drummer boy had looked suddenly enraged.

In the drawing-room Mister Shaw was on his knees beside the General who was down in his chair again. There was such

73

concentration about the fat surgeon's back that, for an instant, Charlie dreaded there'd been a second seizure, more serious than the first.

But the drummer boy's fears proved needless. God knew how he'd come to it, by what tortured means and what crafty suggestion, but Mister Shaw was measuring General Lawrence's gaping mouth for a set of fine false teeth!

'A few days, sir! Only a few days,' promised Mister Shaw as at last they took their departure. 'And you'll be amazed!'

He restrained himself till they were over the threshold, then he could hold himself back no longer. 'I knew it, my dear!' he bubbled. 'I knew we'd do well together! Forty pound I've stung him for! And that's only a beginning ... Charlie! Charlie!'

But the drummer boy didn't answer. He felt he'd left something behind in the house. It frightened and troubled him. It was his heart. Even as dead James Digby before him, he was helplessly, frantically in love with Sophia Lawrence.

IO

MISTER SHAW was in a hurry. He was continually on at the drummer boy to keep up with him.

'Your great gentlemen don't like to be kept waiting!' he panted. 'Always remember that and you'll do all right. They respect prompt attention. After all, it's their due. And I made it clear to the General. He took to me. Had him eating out of my hand, Charlie.' He sniggered. 'But luckily only with his old gnashers! And – and another thing. Never cross 'em, Charlie. They don't like it. I'm not saying you shouldn't stand up to 'em – self-respect and all that – but only till they tell you to sit down. They'll appreciate it, Charlie; and once your great gentleman appreciates you, he won't think twice about bringing you on to his friends. You mayn't believe it, Charlie dear, but he said he might mention me at Court. Oh Charlie! It's another world!'

The fat man was almost crying with pleasure over the fulfilment of his dreams. At last, at last he had his feet on the ladder that would take him out of the filth and blood and darkness in which for so long his talent had been spent. He was coming up into the light of day.

In spite of himself, Charlie was moved by Mister Shaw's longing to better himself. 'And – and will it be best French teeth, like Corporal Finch, for the General?' he asked quite gently, meaning no offence.

But he must have touched on a tender spot. They were crossing Soho Square. Mister Shaw halted and eyed the boy maliciously.

'The enemy's teeth in the General's mouth? God forbid, my dear! It would be treason! Stout English tusks. The very best. I – I'll give him back his own men's teeth! What else? Think of it! When he faces the court martial he'll be able to bare his own men's teeth in defiance; grit them in fortitude and, if the fit's good, gnash them in a rage!'

The surgeon's tiny eyes were winking with spiteful glee. Sick at heart, the drummer boy turned away . . .

'Wait for me – or come in, dear?' Mister Shaw pointed to a shop in Greek Street. *Gamaliel Voice. Teeth fitted for the Trade. Also at Lisle Street.*

Charlie preferred to wait. Mister Shaw looked faintly relieved and waddled into the shop. The drummer boy began to drift up and down the street and round the square, glancing into Mr Voice's window at each passing.

Mister Shaw was perched at a counter, and Mr Voice – a skinny, dusty little man – was examining the surgeon's treasury of teeth, one by one, with a jeweller's glass. Mister Shaw waved – and Charlie passed on.

Some minutes later the situation had improved. Mr Voice had produced a case of mouth plates for Mister Shaw to choose from. Now it was Mister Shaw's turn with the jeweller's glass . . . and Mr Voice waved to the drummer boy.

But when he passed again the situation in the shop had gone quite bizarre. Mr Voice was displaying his range of styles and fittings. Into his lean mouth – which must have been as toothless as a baby's – he fastened sample after sample. Huge bold teeth, little sharp ones fit for ladies, teeth crooked as in nature, mother-of-pearl and agate teeth such as nature never dreamed of; all went into Mr Voice's stretching mouth . . . and grinned flashily at the critical Mister Shaw.

Handsome, handsome – but how secure were they? Mr Voice nodded and picked an apple from a bowl on the counter. Then with each of his wares in turn took a substantial bite.

Mostly, the teeth stayed in his mouth; but now and then a set would be left behind, perched in the apple like a strange mechanical butterfly. Then would Mr Voice give a puzzled smile, and Mister Shaw would gravely shake his head; not that style . . .

76

At last the fat man left the shop and joined Charlie in the sun. The teeth would be ready in four days' time.

It was nearly four o'clock. The sun had all but finished with Soho Square and lingered only in the eastern windows. Already sheets of shadow were being laid across the grass, and

Greek Street was gone quite dark. Some sunshine of the idler sort still stayed about the corners, and here as before, gentlemen congregated as if they'd taken root.

But they were new ones. Already the great town seemed to have changed its inhabitants. Unlike the country where the farmer and his man rise with the sun and are seen growing wearier till at last they're extinguished with the day, the town's life seemed composed of many species who secretly inherited each other's place at secret times. Always bright and new, they decorated the streets, with but the faintest whiff of the furtive to say they'd just left their lairs.

Even the aged contrived to look new. On the corner of Wardour Street a fresh ancient veteran in bleary red had occupied a begging post and blinked alertly as the drummer boy approached.

'Drummed meself for the grand old Dook of Marlborough,' he mumbled, and before Charlie could stir, he'd thumped on the drum with his bony fist. 'Warms the cockles to see you, dear boy. Brings it all back. I was a good-looker, too. God bless you, sir!' This last to a gentleman pushing by and caught fair and square by the old soldier's gnarled and lightning palm.

Then Mister Shaw led Charlie away and they went back to the White Horse. But he did not easily forget the old man; and for the first time it racked his heart that he might tarnish and wrinkle and hobble by the wayside . . . and come to beg in Wardour Street.

'Or will you come with me?' Sophia Lawrence's strange words drifted into his thoughts – and the old man sank like a stone.

They retired early, for the day had been fierce and long; but Sophia Lawrence stood between the drummer boy and sleep. Paler than he remembered her and even more frail. 'We could have saved her,' the General had whispered. Was it already too late?

The troubled drummer boy left his bed and went over and sat by sleeping Mister Shaw. The fat man had an uncanny talent. To Charlie it seemed almost supernatural. But would he use it? Or had he left it behind, in the filth and blood and darkness he'd escaped?

Mister Shaw stirred and sat up. He blinked at the dim face of the drummer boy that had just drawn back from his own.

'What is it, dear?' He reached for his wig, failed to find it and ran his hand hopelessly through his own wretched hair.

'What do you think about her, Mister Shaw?'

The fat man sighed. Said he supposed she was as pretty and good-hearted a girl as might be met with in half an hour's walk anywhere. But he wasn't a judge, really.

Charlie frowned, and continued to do so till it became clear that Mister Shaw was talking about Charity, the maidservant.

'I meant Miss Lawrence, Mister Shaw.'

Mister Shaw compressed his lips. His rouge was smudged and made dark patches under his cheeks, giving him a weirdly hollow air. 'I don't think she'll make old bones, as we say in the trade; if that's what you mean, Charlie.'

His voice was casual, but his eyes were not. He sensed he was in treacherous waters. The drummer boy had gone very pale.

'Then – then she won't live very long?'

'Can't say.' The surgeon had begun fumbling for his wig again. His answer sounded off-hand.

'How long?'

'Ain't a magician, my dear. A year, p'raps; a month . . . p'raps only a week. Then again, I might be wrong –'

'A *week*?' The drummer boy's voice rose sharply. There was a lost and frightened look in his eyes. Through the layers of fat that covered it, the surgeon felt a pang in his heart.

'I ain't certain, my dear. Sometimes these things go on and on and prove the wisest of us fools.'

'What things? What's wrong with her, Mister Shaw?'

'I – I don't know. Only saw her for a moment. Attending the father, y'know. None of my business . . .'

The drummer boy's grief turned to sudden anger. The fat surgeon didn't seem to care whether she lived or died. With difficulty he kept back a retort on what Mister Shaw's business was.

'The court martial. Would – could that kill her . . . as the General said?'

'It won't cure her, and that's for certain sure.'

'But *you* could, Mister Shaw, couldn't you?'

The boy's eyes burned into Mister Shaw's – and the fat man

shrank back among his bedclothes. He had been taken quite unawares; and the drummer boy pursued him relentlessly.

The drummer boy's faith in the surgeon's genius was merciless in its scope. He crouched by his bed, his young face frantic with hope. In vain Mister Shaw tried to ward him off – to escape his pleading – to disengage himself from the consequence of talent. But the drummer boy had hooked him by the very soul, and the harder he tugged, the worse the pain.

'I love her, Mister Shaw – with all my heart and with all my soul and with all my might!'

'But – but does she know it –?'

'I – I think so. I kissed her . . .'

The fat man started – drew in his breath harshly. 'For God's sake!' he began; then changed his mind and asked Charlie gently if he'd forgotten that Sophia Lawrence was a general's daughter, while he . . . But the drummer boy had not forgotten. Love, no less than death, was a great leveller. And that was something Mister Shaw seemed to have forgotten.

'She asked me to come with her, Mister Shaw,' said Charlie triumphantly.

The fat man's eyes widened – but he did not answer. The drummer boy's words seemed to have taken his breath away. He scowled and went back to his search for his wig. At last he found it and put it on. It was newish and fashionable, but on Mister Shaw it looked like a large dead bird. Though he'd a passion for fancy clothes, they became him no better than did his other passions. Mister Shaw was a man at odds with himself – and always the loser.

'So . . . will you help me?'

'Yes,' said the surgeon suddenly. 'I'll help you. Never go to Bruton Street again. There. That's the best I can do for you.'

'And the cheapest, too!' The drummer boy had stood up. Rage and bitterness was in his face. 'Would it be the same if I could pay, Master Shaw?'

'You – you don't understand –'

'I *do* understand! I understand you hate love. You hate anything where there's no profit!'

'I hate love?' The fat man stared at him incredulously. 'Oh God, Charlie – do you know what love is? It ain't just the spitting flicker of green wood catching. It's a mighty weapon, Charlie! It's the defender of the faith – it's the only thing we still have on our side! Even my talent, Charlie, only exists because of love! It's – Charlie! Where are you going?'

The boy had begun to dress in a furious, feverish fashion. Helplessly the surgeon pleaded with him to wait, consider . . . But he might as easily have tried to oppose a whirlwind with blowing. The drummer boy wanted to get out into the night. The oppression of the room was suffocating him. It stank of death and decay.

'Come back, Charlie –'

The boy had snatched up his beloved drum and opened the door. 'You was right, Mister Shaw, when you said love's the only thing on our side. It's the only thing *I've* got – besides me drum. But by heaven, I want to use it before I'm kippered! I'll save her, Mister Shaw. I ain't going to lose her just on your say-so!'

With that, he was gone. Mister Shaw heard him clattering down the stairs. He went to the window; saw the drummer boy running across the street. He struggled to open the window. He wanted to call after him. There was something else he wanted to tell him, something fearful and strange that concerned such a dream of love as the drummer boy's for the dying general's daughter. It was something that had haunted the surgeon all his life, and now it stood horribly clear. But he could not get the window open; and the boy had vanished into the night.

II

THERE seemed to be an invisible, riderless horse plunging through the streets and dragging Charlie in its wake. It panted and clashed on the cobbles even as he did in his flight.

Confused thoughts rushed through his mind; strange sharp memories of his childhood, forest days and forest nights, the bellowing day he joined the army, and then at the end of it all, the beggar of Wardour Street: 'I was a good-looker once.'

Bruton Street. His steps echoed stonily, and the dark houses seemed to be holding their knockers to their black lips. The drummer boy slowed down. His breath came hard and harsh. Ahead was the shadowy square. Westward stood a half-built house: its ragged walls rose against the sky as if they'd been half eaten by the sharp stars. Even heaven was full of teeth . . .

The invisible horse that had dragged him hither seemed to have gone – perhaps to feed among the quiet trees. Why had it brought him to this place? He peered towards the trees as if the answer lay there. He did not look towards the General's house. Something prevented him, even seemed to be warning him that such a look might well be the end of him. He felt a strong impulse to abandon the place while his eyes were still averted. But he could not. He turned –

God in Heaven! What was it? Blood. There seemed to be a gigantic clot of blood clinging to the house's face!

It was the ghost. Like a smear of red, it hung from Sophia's window, seeking to get in. The drummer boy cried out – and it was gone.

He shook with terror that it was within the house; then he heard it whisper: 'Let me have her, Charlie. She's mine . . .' Where was it? Close at hand. Behind him? Beside him? The phantom was in his drum.

'Don't save her. Let her come to me . . . We will be outcasts together. Don't save her . . . don't . . .'

The voice was thin and wailing. It begged and pleaded; called him 'Charlie' and 'dear friend'.

'I love her!' groaned the drummer boy. 'Leave us! Leave us in peace!'

'Let me have her, my friend. Don't save her . . .'

Desperately he tried to shut out the phantom's urging. He put his fingers to his ears – but the voice penetrated flesh and bone as easily as it pierced the air. So he tried the drum. Softly (for it was between midnight and dawn) he tapped . . . and to his joyous relief the voice sank away under the military muttering.

Once more the drum had conquered death. Exultantly the drummer boy fancied the phantom had shrieked and fled from it and all its mighty memories. He played on . . . no Funeral Retreat but the haughty, high-stepping Advance. He played to the quiet dark house – and kept the ghost at bay.

Suddenly the door opened. A figure, cloaked and hooded, glided out and crossed the street. The drummer boy's heart thundered louder than his instrument. The figure approached.

'For pity's sake, give over that grisly row, Charlie Samson!' It was Charity, the maidservant. 'D'you want to wake the dead?' Her face attracted a deal of starlight. It shone with humorous reproach. She fidgeted her feet and her shift or petticoat poked out impudently.

Charlie stared at her in angry disappointment. She frowned and said sharply that it was time for all soldier boys to be abed and having their beauty sleep.

'Damn you!' said Charlie. 'I'm not a child, miss!'

She looked at him. 'You're well enough grown, that I'll grant. Real handsome in a country style. But – but then so are some children.'

Charlie scowled. 'I've lived through more than ever you can dream of, miss.'

'Charity,' murmured she. 'The name's Charity –'

'I've marched into battle,' went on the drummer boy with grim pride. 'I've seen tremendous men shriek and fall and die all round me. I've sounded the Funeral Retreat over ten thousand dead. I've –'

'All right!' she interrupted. 'I don't doubt your adventures, my lad. But there's more to being a man than marching about in his boots!' She stopped. Her pert young face had gone suddenly serious. 'Charlie – dear Charlie, leave this place. Go home and – and don't come back no more. Don't you see? The house is falling down – and you can't prop it up with a pair of drumsticks!'

'Is it – is it the court martial?'

'Among other things. Too many for a drummer boy.'

'I'll take me chances, miss.'

'What's the matter? Why "miss"? Don't you care for Charity?' She smiled. 'Remember what it says; though you speak with the tongues of angels, you ain't up to much if you're without Charity!'

'When I want Charity, I'll ask –'

'Beg, you mean!' The girl's eyes flashed angrily; then she went on, 'Please leave us. Miss Sophia's not for you. She's –'

'She's what?'

'They say she's not long for this world, Charlie Samson.'

'That's not for certain!'

'If it's a rich catch you're after, I've got twenty pound myself. And a very loving nature!'

Her face peeping out from her hood looked mocking, though her voice was tender. But the drummer boy was too deep in his whirlpool of love for Sophia, and the more he heard of her uneasy tenure of life, the fiercer grew his resolve to save her. Perhaps no one, save Sophia herself, understood the wild, desperate nature of this love, and what it might achieve. Almost pityingly he looked at Charity and said, 'She – she asked me to come with her, you know . . .'

At once the girl drew back. She glanced up to her mistress's window and even in the faint starlight the expression on her face was plain. It was a look of hatred and loathing.

'You fool! Don't you knows what she means?'

She shivered, drew her cloak about her, thereby extinguishing her petticoat, and went back quickly into the house.

He took up a place on the corner of the square opposite the General's house. He returned only briefly to the White Horse when he could no longer keep awake and had to sleep or fall where he stood. He grew pale and hollow-eyed, and excited even the mute's apprehensive pity.

At first he inconvenienced a pair of veterans from some mysterious battle (perhaps it was only life?) who begged nearby. But soon they found him quite an attraction to the passing trade and begged quite prosperously behind his firm young back. They shared their food with him; but he ate very little. Once or twice Mister Shaw attempted to draw him away, but the drummer boy would not leave his post. He was guarding the house against the return of the ghost.

His eyes were turned, with painful intensity, to the window high up, behind which was his strange love.

He never crossed the street nor attempted more than his unceasing stare. There was no need. From time to time a face of astonishing beauty would appear at the window and look down on the drummer boy. Then he would smile and faintly raise a drumstick in salute. The face would linger awhile . . . as if caught in as strong toils as was the drummer boy himself.

Sometimes, in the mornings, Charity would come out and hasten by on some errand for her mistress. But she never spoke to the drummer boy; only looked back at him when she'd passed . . . perhaps surprised by how pale he'd grown and how deep were sunk his eyes. Once she hesitated – then shook her head with a troubled air.

For three days he kept the ghost away. But he could not hold off the other enemy – the gathering clouds of the General's fall that would destroy Sophia as surely as a knife in her heart.

Carriages called; the thin grey minister came several times, and with him others, stern-faced, bearing documents. Once another general came and went up the steps like a little bonfire of stars and orders. But he, like the others, didn't stay long – and came out no better pleased than when he'd gone in. It seemed that none of them was getting any change out of General Lawrence.

Sooner or later, however, they would bring the huge man tumbling down. The boy watched them with desolate hatred; but they were not susceptible to his shining drum. There was no Advance that would hold *them* off.

On the afternoon of the third day the fading drummer boy became aware that passers-by were loitering, sometimes in small groups, and staring at the house curiously, expectantly. Even the mute was put out and glanced uneasily upward as if the watchers had seen a crack in the house's face that betokened its imminent fall.

They were like those creatures in whom nature has implanted so keen a sense of impending death that they can smell it out over vast distances. Somehow, they'd heard of the magnitude of the General's crime and they were waiting for him to shoot himself rather than answer for it. None of them seriously expected to see it happen, but all hoped to hear the shot.

It was on the evening of that day that Charlie Samson saw James Digby's spectre for the last time but one. At first he thought it was a lonely watcher, moving behind him. Then came the appalling sense of the broken head just behind his own and a curious tingling smell that recalled spent powder, only sweeter . . .

'You cannot stop them, my friend. They'll bring him down and then the thread of her life will snap. She will be mine . . . mine . . . Perhaps tomorrow . . . perhaps in a week. It is very soon now. You must go away, Charlie, my friend, and leave all to me.'

'No!' whispered the drummer boy. 'So long as I'm alive I'll try to save her!'

'With a pair of drumsticks?'

'There – there's another way!' The drummer boy's voice was low and trembling. For the first time he'd betrayed something that he'd kept in the darkest part of his mind. And it was something he feared as much as he feared the ghost. But now there was nothing else left to him.

'There is no other way! Not for you!' The phantom sounded alarmed. 'Remember . . . remember . . .'

'There is another way. And I must take it.'

'Then God help you, my dear friend. God help you . . .'

12

SATURDAY, June third. An enormous sun began to lift above the rooftops and sweep away the soiling of the night. It swept it up into dirty black shadows and left it outside the houses on one side of each street. These shadows were cold and musty to walk in and the surgeon and the drummer boy shivered as they hastened on.

Mister Shaw had risen terrifically early to call on Mr Voice and get the General's teeth. It was the fat man's day of fulfilment, the day that was to lift him clear of his unlucky past.

They crossed Soho Square and stepped into the part the sun had cleaned. At once they blazed and Charlie's drum flashed golden and hurt the surgeon's eyes. Then Mister Shaw was extinguished in Greek Street and Charlie gazed blindly at the sky. A single wisp of cloud hung high above Carlisle Street.

'If no more clouds come, then all will go well,' murmured the boy; then he started. Why had he said that? The thought had come unbidden. Was he being warned that all was decided in the sky . . . and quite out of his power? He shook his head. He believed too firmly in his own strength and in the dangerous way he'd decided on. Nonetheless he continued to watch the sky and felt a great relief when the wisp of cloud departed and left the sky quite clean.

Then Mister Shaw came out and showed him Mr Voice's craftsmanship. Never had the teeth from the hillside looked so bright and neat. Set in tinted ivory, they smiled in the sun; seven in the upper row and four in the lower, with spiders' threads of gold to anchor them in the General's mouth.

There was another set, too, planted in untarnishable pewter. They were large, even ungainly, but so lifelike that they looked as if they might bite of their own accord. They were French and for Corporal Finch. They were almost a portrait of him – so skilfully had Mister Shaw measured him up and noted him down. If not a speaking likeness, they were certainly an eating likeness of the great gaunt corporal.

They reached Bruton Street at about ten o'clock. Already the inquisitive watchers were gathering. Would it be today?

At first, the mute was inclined to deny Mister Shaw; then the fat man gave him a shilling and he blessed Mister Shaw for coming again. 'And may you be at my door afore I'm at your'n.'

Visitors were already with the General, and the footman who answered the door had a flustered look. As he crossed the threshold the drummer boy glanced up at the sky. Still no clouds . . .

'Expecting me,' confided Mister Shaw to the footman. 'Matter of importance.'

The air within was sharp and restless, with the smell of snuff. From time to time candles jumped and sparked as they caught drifting grains and sneezed them up.

A murmur of voices was coming from the drawing-room. The footman hesitated on the stair.

'Matter of importance!' repeated Mister Shaw; but the footman still hesitated. Then from aloft the drummer boy heard a voice whisper, 'Charlie Samson – Charlie Samson, come to me.'

Though it was soft, it was very clear . . . and it seemed extraordinary at the time that neither the footman nor Mister Shaw gave sign of having heard it.

Mister Shaw tried to seize him and the footman called out; but the drummer boy had mounted out of their reach. He looked down on them with angry bewilderment. Hadn't they heard he'd been called?

The door of the little parlour was shut. Hurriedly he knocked, fearing pursuit.

'Yes?'

'You called me. It's Charlie Samson . . .'

'I called you? When?'

'Just now . . .'

The door opened and Charity stood looking at him. Her face was angry and frightened. She glanced back over her shoulder. Her mistress was on the couch by the window. She was nodding and smiling. Charity bit her lip and left the room without a word. But her face lingered in the drummer boy's mind.

'So I called you?'

'Yes. I heard you . . .'

She shook her head and her taffeta shawl rustled like dead leaves. But her colour had improved and her eyes shone as if a fresh source of life had been kindled within her. A feeling of great joy filled the drummer boy. The surgeon had been wrong.

She beckoned him to come nearer, which he gladly did, and squatted on his drum beside his weird wild love.

Gravely she thanked him for his serenade in the square of the other night. No; he'd not wakened her. She slept little and the sound of the drum in the night had reminded her of all he'd said about the hillside. Then she reproached him for growing so pale – most especially as she herself seemed to be gaining in strength.

'See,' she said, taking up a looking-glass and showing it to him. 'You fade while I bloom. It should not be so, drummer boy. We – we should bloom together . . . for we are both young.'

The drummer boy looked – and was amazed by the sunken youth who stared back at him with lost and frightened eyes.

'Am I taking your life away?' she murmured, and her voice itself seemed to hold a rustle within it as if her heart was wrapped in night-black taffeta. 'For since you came – since you've stood outside, I've got stronger. Everyone is surprised. I – I think they expected me to – to die, you know.' Here she smiled in a curiously ashamed way, and the drummer boy's heart ached with pity and passion. 'But I'm not going to die now.'

Suddenly she was bending close to him. The sweetness in the air grew strong and heady. Once again it was overpowering the boy. Her lips moved; her words were scarcely audible. 'Why – why do you want to save me?'

He looked at her in painful desperation – and then his bewildered young love could no longer be held back.

'Because I love you!' he cried, and saw her face, dark against the bright window, look down on him almost enviously.

Something warm struck his cheek and briefly seemed to burn. Sophia was crying. Silently, helplessly, tears were falling from her eyes. 'I'm frightened – so frightened!' she whispered. 'I saw two old men begging behind your back ... and I thought one of them was you, and it broke my heart. We are dreams, Charlie. We are dreams of love and youth and beauty. We mustn't lose each other! Oh Charlie – I'm so frightened! Save me ... please save me!'

He longed to tell her that that was why he had come, that he was going to save her; but he could not bring himself to tell her how. Instead, he nodded.

'You promise? You *will* save me?'

He stood up, put on his drum and went to the door. He looked back. She was sitting with her back to the sunlight. Her hair was like black fire. 'Promise ... promise ...'

Beyond her the sky was bright. There was not a cloud in all the heavens. 'I promise.'

'Or will you come with me?' Had she spoken the words – or were they but an echo in the boy's mind? Her face was in shadow; her expression unclear. Yet its very darkness seemed to hold a triumphant smile.

The General had got his teeth in. They were a great success. The scarlet men would have been proud to know they hadn't been altogether wasted. Mister Shaw regarded him with satisfaction and the General's eyes kept straying to the mirror over the mantel. He looked twenty years younger – in his prime – and he longed to go upstairs and smile at his beautiful younger daughter.

If there was any criticism of Mr Voice's work it was that the tinted ivory presented itself too much and gave the General the curious appearance of having a second, secret tongue.

He'd not attempted to eat with them yet, there were visitors present; and these visitors were even more threatening and unpleasant than before. He felt they were closing in on him and that the decency imposed by the presence of the widow and the 'personal items' was reaching its limit.

He made a point of never receiving but in the room of mourning. He was very strict about that. Whenever he heard the front door he hurried in and claimed the sanctuary of respect for the bereaved. But now it was become quite plain that this could not go on for much longer. Even the widow sensed it. Pale and strained, she gazed at the thin grey minister who was letting her son play with the fob of his watch. From time to time he looked up, caught her eye and shrugged his shoulders.

'I – really don't blame you, sir,' the General was saying to a colleague who'd called before. 'I blame no one. We are all victims . . .'

His colleague was a little general with a face like a nutcracker. He was taking snuff. Pinch after pinch of it. His aide watched him uneasily, as if his master was charging his fierce little head and any moment it would go off.

'I think we have heard enough, gentlemen; quite enough. I demand a warrant this afternoon. This – this man must be arrested. I see no evidence to support him. Nothing whatsoever.'

On the word 'nothing', General Lawrence began to crumple. He clutched at his heart. Mister Shaw reached forward.

'I – I am not a well man, gentlemen –'

'I can think of ten thousand even less well!'

'You cannot blame me –'

'Who else?'

'Blame, blame! Why must we always turn to blame? What good does it do? Can it bring my brave men back? If so, then blame me, gentlemen! Court martial me directly and give the widows back their husbands. Yes – give my daughter back Fitzwarren himself. But don't blame him for what he unluckily did! Don't blame him, gentlemen. His crime was weakness more than cowardice. A father-in-law pleads. Spare him!'

'Good God! The way this man wriggles! Let me tell you, sir, nobody is going to blame a dead man for your offence! Nobody but you ever thought of it. Nobody but you heard the order – if such an order was ever given!'

'*He* heard it! *He* heard it!' shouted General Lawrence. 'Fitzwarren heard it!'

At last panic had seized hold on the General's mind. A horrible panic like a quicksand from which there was neither advance nor retreat. He turned and turned – and his accusers watched him implacably. 'You – you have my word . . . there's nothing else . . . The order – I swear he heard it –'

But no one answered. Bewildered, the General discovered no one was attending him. They were staring to the door.

'I – heard – it – too.'

Who'd spoken? What angel had come to his defence? Disbelievingly the General peered about him. Then he grinned with all his soldiers' teeth. In the doorway stood the drummer boy!

Very rigid and upright, with his great glinting drum at his knee, looking for all the world as if he'd just come from the glorious dead to give his evidence. He was the very spirit of the fallen, and in the candlelight he seemed to shine. Even to the world-weary minister it was plain he was the golden lad . . . and his word would carry the heavy weight of gold.

In vain the nutcracker general raged and fumed and made

to fly at him with all the mighty consequence of rank; but even he fell back helplessly before the advancing drummer boy. What was his savage old annoyance before this fierce pale youth? So the old man retreated, muttering, 'Lies! Lies! You put him up to it! All lies –'

But if one old man was in retreat, the other was in full advance, galloping on with banners streaming and pale eyes aflame. 'Lies?' shouted General Lawrence, catching sight of himself in the polished drum. 'You dare to call this splendid lad a liar? This lad from the terrible hillside? This hero come back from the dead?' He'd grabbed hold of Charlie's arm as if alarmed that his saviour might change his mind and make off. 'Look at him!' He pulled the boy into the middle of the room. 'If you doubt him, you doubt the glorious dead! Oh gentlemen, gentlemen, don't cast doubt on our country's dead! Court martial me if you will, but spare the brave dead! Their General pleads . . . spare the memory of the dead! My boy, my dear boy, just you tell them again – *in trumpet tones* – that I was ever true!'

The General was smiling down on him. His teeth gleamed and swam before Charlie's eyes till he had the wild notion that they were about to leap out of the General's mouth and tear and bite him for betraying their first possessors. But overriding all was the memory of Sophia's 'I'm frightened – so frightened –'

'I heard you give the order to Major Fitzwarren to search the wood. And I saw – saw he never went . . . and lied to you. I saw it all. I swear it.'

The room seemed to shrink away from him. With his word alone he'd conquered. Of a sudden, he knew the terrible strength there lay in it. It bridged the quicksand, it crossed the whirlpool.

'Trust,' grinned General Lawrence, in full military command. 'There comes a time, eh, gentlemen, when there's nothing else, eh? And by God! there's no one I'd sooner trust than this innocent shining drummer boy!'

Then Charlie Samson chanced to see Mister Shaw. The fat seedy surgeon was sitting down. He was gazing at his drummer boy and his mean and piggy eyes were running over with tears.

Everyone had begun to talk again. The General was extraordinarily affable. He kept patting Charlie's shoulder and affectionately tapping his drum. 'Samson, eh? Samson! Well, well! There was once a Samson who pulled a mansion down; but here's another who's held one up!' Then he bent low and murmured, 'It's more than me you've saved! Oh yes, much, much more!' And he glanced upward – and smiled.

Behind the huge, red man, Charlie could see the black curtains. They were not quite drawn. Sunlight like a sword blade divided them. The sky had kept clear for him. The heavens had kept *their* word.

'Just one thing more.' The nutcracker general and the minister had been together. It was the minister who'd spoken. He'd given the widow's child a sixpence to let go of his watch fob. He'd made quite a success with the little boy and was plainly pleased about it. He was smiling . . .

'Nothing of any importance, you understand. Please don't misunderstand me. I'm not doubting. Fully appreciate the value of a word . . . and *such* a word.' He nodded to Charlie. 'But just to be certain – in this uncertain world! – that we won't be wasting the court's time, could the lady identify Major Fitzwarren? These miniatures – several, I see, and one of the Major. Excellent likeness.' He picked one up, then laughed mischievously. 'No, not that one. Mustn't give it away, eh? Come, young man! A moment's glance will be enough. After all, you remember so much surely you can remember which was the man you saw the General give his order to? Which one of these miniatures is of Major Fitzwarren?'

The sword of sunlight suddenly seemed to be blinding the boy. He faltered; he grew cold; he could scarcely see. The damned minister had destroyed him. He had never set eyes on

Major Fitzwarren in his life. He had not the faintest hope of picking on the right miniature.

General Lawrence was leading him, pulling him towards the table. The minister waited; and over his shoulder grinned the devilish face of the nutcracker general.

Someone had moved. The widow. She had gone from the room. Uninterrupted, the sword of sunlight fell across the table and the 'personal items' blazed as if with vengeful fire.

Charlie had no choice but to continue. The General's grip was hard on his arm. He put out a hand. He heard the nutcracker general hiss with expection. He took up the nearest picture. Shook his head. It had been of a lady – perhaps the dead man's mother. He put it back and took another. A brisk young officer smirked sideways at him; but the General's grip stayed tight. He shook his head again – and the General's fingers loosened in relief.

'Stand clear, sir,' muttered the nutcracker general. 'No assistance if you please.'

Reluctantly General Lawrence let go of Charlie's arm. The boy almost fell. His last hope had left him.

His hand weighed so heavy he could scarcely move it. But he reached again. The third portrait was of another officer, but of Marlborough's day. Unluckily for Charlie, the Major's family had been military to a man. Came another, sitting in an Italian garden. Was it he? Certainly he had a weak and furtive look about him. Such a man might well have murdered ten thousand with a lie. He hesitated – and the General held his breath. Then he saw the sunlight glint fierily on another frame, A pretty silver frame with a design of grapes and leaves, such as might have held the portrait of a young girl.

Impulsively he reached for it. Stared at it. His mouth dried up. A great wind seemed to roar through his head.

'This – is – the – man,' he whispered.

The minister had been right. The likeness was an excellent one. Out of the frame there smiled the face of Maddox!

13

'DON'T go to Bruton Street!' Maddox's words howled and screamed in his mind – and for the first time he heard the terror that lay in them. Maddox, the haunted man. Ten thousand deaths on his conscience!

Memory after memory piled one on another till Maddox's agony stood pitilessly clear. He'd fled from the hillside, but could not leave it behind. He'd changed coats with a dead man, changed names with a street – to leave himself behind. But neither could he do that.

'Did you lose a brother?' What a thing to ask a man who'd lost ten thousand! 'Take it to remind you. Souvenir of the gurr.' Much he needed reminding. How the dark sea must have beckoned him . . .

But then to be saved from it – to be dragged back mercilessly to what he'd screwed up his courage to escape! Maddox! Face glazed with tears; fearful of all company – and most afraid of his own . . . from which there seemed no escape.

Dazed with pity, Charlie Samson prayed that the unlucky man would come to find peace in the forest; hidden . . . secure . . .

'This man is still alive.' Mister Shaw had taken the miniature from the drummer boy's hand. His face had gone grey under his rouge and his flabby cheeks shook. But his voice was firm to the point of harshness. 'You don't need the boy's evidence. I know where this man is.'

'Don't – don't –'

But the fat man was as hard as stone, and his little eyes glittered like diamonds. What was Maddox to him beside the gratitude of a minister and another general? They turned from the drummer boy and gathered round the fat man. Smiles, astonishment, expectation danced in their cold eyes and stretched their old cracked lips.

'I can take you to him . . .'

The boy was retreating, shrinking away from the greedy fat man who was pawing the silver frame. Suddenly he gave a cry of despair and fled from the room.

'Let him go!' pleaded Mister Shaw. 'He'll not go far – I'll answer for him. He will be back. He has no money, you see . . .'

No one stopped him, no one followed him as he stumbled away from the house. The silent watchers saw him, pale and singularly wild-eyed – and wondered if all was over. Perhaps the General had hanged himself and cheated them out of the shot?

The sun blazed mockingly in a cloudless sky. The heavens had kept their word. Charlie cursed them for it. Clouds as red as blood should have filled the sky to warn him of what lay beyond success.

Maddox had foreseen it. Maddox had pleaded with him, as if he'd seen in the drummer boy's eyes the image of revenge. The unforgiving drummer boy who'd dragged him back from finding peace in the sea . . . and would just as surely prevent him finding peace in the forest. The drummer boy whose golden word had become a scourge.

He stumbled and ran through street after street with a single hope remaining. The forest, the forest! If only he could reach it before the others! If only he could reach Maddox and warn him.

But Mister Shaw had been right. He'd not enough money to get him to the end of Piccadilly.

Suddenly he found himself in Wardour Street. Rich men and women passed to and fro. Many were the kindly looks they gave him. But would they give him more? He stopped. He held out his hand. 'God bless you, sir, if you can help me?'

A shilling fell on his drum. The boy snatched it up. 'God bless you, sir, if you can help me . . .?'

They passed by, the merchants and gentlemen and their glimmering wives. Kindly looks turned harder, but here and there turned to pity . . . and they dropped their silver tears on the pale young soldier's drum. Then a child came by and did him proud. Three sixpences. It had chuckled at the rattle of the money on the drumskin, and its father took pleasure in its laughter.

The ancient fellow who'd drummed for Marlborough shook his fist from across the street, and cursed his young rival for taking the bread out of his mouth.

Now came an elegant young man of principle who didn't hold with begging. But he was willing to give the drummer boy a guinea – a whole guinea – if he'd play a tune. So Charlie Samson obliged and played. He played the Retreat – but not for the fallen. He played it for himself. Of all the scarlet men, he, their golden lad, had fallen the farthest. As he tapped and rattled away for the gentlemen of Wardour Street, tears were streaming down his cheeks. A perjurer and a beggar . . . The guinea dropped on his drum. 'God bless you, sir –'

At last he'd got enough. His ordeal was over and he ran from Wardour Street like a thief. He went back to the White Horse and boarded the first coach bound for the West.

Mister Shaw was not happy. He was being rushed. The General was in a military ecstasy. Fitzwarren must be taken at once, directly – before he'd time to escape to God knew where.

The household was like a regiment striking camp – movement and noise everywhere and the curious, faintly oily smell that rises up when an army stirs.

The visitors had gone, but the nutcracker general had left his aide behind – almost as a keepsake. This smooth young man, with rosy cheeks and starfish eyes was forever getting in the way. Wherever he tucked himself, he was always jostling the General's eye. 'Oh yes, and you, sir!' The General snapped irritably whenever he caught sight of him.

A pair of carriages were summoned and a detachment of footmen in the expectation of Fitzwarren's offering resistance. Impatiently the General urged haste – more haste – and in mirror after mirror his huge form took on a fiercer shine. He was full of youthful energy, even as in the days of his courtship when he carried all before him.

'Papa!'

He turned. A troubled look broke up his face ... then he smiled. Sophia had come down. She stood on the stair and gazed at her magnificent father. Her face burned with excitement and almost passionate admiration.

'My child! You should not be –'

'I'm better, Papa! To see you so is – is worth all the physicians!'

The General glanced proudly at Mister Shaw then expanded his chest towards his dearest child. 'An adventure, my darling. We're off on a little adventure. Fitzwarren – alive! We're going to find him. In the New Forest. Hunt the Major, eh?'

'May I come with you, sir? Will you take me? So long upstairs ... it's so dull ... Please let me come with you! To see you – to watch you ...'

'But, my child – the carriage – it's not comfortable – scarce room ... what with myself, this good surgeon and – and –' He saw the rosy aide in a corner. He scowled. 'Oh yes, and you, sir!'

But whatever he might say, it was plain the General was supernaturally excited by the prospect of performing before his wonderfully beautiful child. He applied to Mister Shaw for reassurance that the journey would do her no harm.

Uneasily, Mister Shaw disclaimed. He was no physician. The General urged. Mister Shaw shrugged his shoulders. Yes, he had some knowledge in that direction, but ... An opinion, then! Mister Shaw sighed – and gave one. The journey would make no difference, one way or the other.

Impulsively the General thanked him. He had been too occupied in seeing himself in his radiant daughter to observe much of the fat man's expression or tone of voice. There had been nothing to be thankful for in either.

At last they were ready. Six footmen were in the second carriage with, surprisingly, a quantity of muskets. The General and his willing helper, the surgeon, were to travel in the first carriage together with Sophia and her maid. There was no room for the aide. Absolutely none. Either he travelled on the box beside the coachman or he stayed behind. He might please himself. The aide blinked his starfish eyes and elected for the box. He was in no position to please himself.

They were gathered in the hall, waiting on Sophia and her maid, when Mister Shaw remembered the drummer boy. Though he suspected the boy had set off for the Forest, there was yet a possibility he'd returned to the inn. Humbly he begged the General to allow him to send some money to the White Horse for Charlie Samson's needs.

At once General Lawrence was a tower of concern. The drummer boy must be preserved at all costs. His word – his golden word – would yet be needed in court.

'But you will have the Major himself –'

'Ah!' said the General, squeezing his hands into white gloves and trying to observe his own profile in the nearest mirror. 'The Major. Yes, indeed. But – but what if he should escape us? Where are we then – without the drummer boy and his word?' He nodded sagely and tapped his heart. 'Reserves, sir. A good general considers reserves.'

'But if we secure Maddox – er – Fitzwarren, what then?'

The General frowned. He beckoned Mister Shaw and bent close. His teeth snapped and clicked at the surgeon's ear. 'Hardly care to say this of the father of my grandson, but what if he denies everything? Eh? Not that I'd blame him, poor fellow . . . but where would we be without the drummer boy and his golden word? The word, sir, the word. All gives way before it. Swords, muskets, all the fierce apparatus of war is as nothing before the word. If Fitzwarren denies, then truth itself is defeated; unless there is another word in reserve. Yes, yes – we must send money to the drummer boy!'

He drew back and straightened a bouquet of crepe that perched above the mirror. He glanced round the darkened hall where crepe pennants flew across the panels. He sighed. Another thought had struck him. 'In a way it would have been better if – if the poor fellow had found peace on the battlefield. After all, we mourn him now. Much distress would have been avoided. The spectacle of Fitzwarren denying his father-in-law's word. Which will come! This I know. I understand him as well as I know myself. He'll deny everything, and – and –'

He stopped. His daughter and her maid were coming down the stairs. The General seemed to put on an extra glitter. Sophia smiled. He pushed a footman aside and opened the door for her himself. Sunlight streamed inside and, for a moment, seemed to consume her. Then a black shadow crossed her. It was the inquisitive, unnecessary mute. She stared at him, momentarily frightened. Why was he still there? Was he an omen? The mute looked at her in startled admiration. She blushed and rustled down the steps towards the carriage. The mute's eyes followed her with melancholy longing.

Now came the General and Mister Shaw. There was an audible sigh of dashed hopes from the watchers across the street. The General frowned. He could not quite understand how he could be the cause of anyone's disappointment.

He looked back at his house. The knocker was still wrapped in crepe; the mute still waited; and above him, black and grim, was the hatchment that proclaimed the death of Major Fitzwarren. He opened his mouth, then shut it tight and went to his carriage. He glanced at the second carriage. The armed footmen were within. He nodded, then peered up at his coachman. He scowled. 'Oh yes, and you, sir!' he muttered as he saw the aide; and climbed rapidly inside.

He had given no order for the hatchment to be removed nor for the mute to be dismissed. Yet it had seemed that he'd been on the point of doing so. What deep instinct or intention had prevented him? Mister Shaw stared at him. The General began to feel uncomfortable. He looked for his reflection in the carriage window. Was anything amiss with his appearance? The fat fellow had looked at him as if he'd spied something almost ugly. But the General could see nothing wrong and so troubled his soldierly mind no further. 'That drummer boy,' he murmured, more to himself than to Mister Shaw, 'we must look after him. One never knows what might happen in a place like the forest, eh?'

They began to move away. Mister Shaw stared fretfully out of the window. He seemed to be trying to creep inside his own shell of fat. He was racked with misery. His love for the drummer boy had dragged him into darker places than any he'd sought to escape. Suddenly he understood he was become the flabby accomplice of a man resolved on murder. There was no doubt that General Lawrence hoped to kill his son-in-law rather than risk that wretched man's defending himself.

He, Mister Shaw, surgeon, was even more loathsome in his own sight than usual. He shuddered and glanced enviously at the General whose love for his daughter seemed, by contrast, almost inspiring.

Money and success. They were the only things left to Mister Shaw. He clenched his fleshy hands till the nails bit into his palms. Whatever happened, he must hold on . . .

At four o'clock, in dying sunshine, they passed the apple stall at Hyde Park Corner. They were just three and a half hours behind the public coach that had carried the drummer boy.

14

THE benefit of fine weather was turning sour from excess of it. Already the earth had forgotten the previous month's downpours and the farmers were in a panic from lack of rain. Two trades alone welcomed the parching dryness. Innkeeping prospered on account of water being scarcer than ale; and the public coaches clipped hours off journeys along the hard dry roads.

The coach that came into Ringwood at midday on June fifth was four hours ahead of its time. Nonetheless, the desperate-looking drummer boy it had carried scrambled down and fled away as if, whatever the time, he was already too late.

Throughout the journey he'd sat in a corner as if he'd been trying to creep inside himself. From time to time he'd polished his drum on his sleeve, but it seemed it wouldn't come clean. The boy kept frowning at it . . . then he'd resume his aspect of sunken dismay so that the coachman had real fears that he was considering making away with himself. Which would have been a pity as the lad was young and still had much to commend him . . .

The forest was full of noises. Obscure tickings and chatterings disturbed the trees, and everywhere there was a dry, harsh rustling.

The red-coated figure of the drummer boy moved swiftly among the trees, sometimes blazing out like a sunburst as he stepped across a patch of light and the sun caught on his drum; then changing to a vague touch of scarlet among the speckled brown and green.

At last he reached the gypsies' huts. They were deserted.

'Maddox! Maddox!' he called softly. No reply. Only the ceaseless rustling above, beside and all about him.

'Corporal Finch! Mushoo! Edwards, Parsons!' Nothing. The leaves shook and a capacious oak groaned and crackled under the broken sun.

The boy began to grow alarmed. He feared some Revenue disaster had overtaken them all and whisked them off.

He tapped on his drum. Softly he played and the drum beats began to echo mysteriously through the forest. Strange configurations of branch and trunk caught the sound and threw it back, and to the boy it seemed that the huge still trees were beginning to stir and dance to the beating of the drum. Even the great oak seemed to be shuddering. All its leaves were quivering and, with a harsh sound, it spread its branches and disgorged its scarlet soul.

'Finch,' it said, as it dropped to the ground. 'By the grace of God a corporal an' still surviving.'

Parsons come out of an empty thicket and Mushoo drifted out of the very air. The boy stared at them in amazement, till he remembered they were all prodigies of concealment – which was why they'd stayed alive.

'The warrior lad's come back,' said gaunt Corporal Finch with honest pleasure; then asked after his gnashers.

'Maddox,' muttered Charlie. 'Where's Maddox?'

The corporal didn't know. Maddox went off during the days. Picking bluebells, for all the corporal knew. He never came back till nightfall. What did the warrior lad want with him?

Charlie Samson gazed at the pleased survivors. They gathered about him half sepulchred in twigs and leaves – even as when first they'd met.

'I – I must warn him. Men are coming – coming for him.'

Who? How many? When? The smiles melted from the survivors' faces. They looked to one another. They began to back away. Discretion being the better part of valour, none of them was inclined to be caught with the rubbish. If they saw Maddox, they'd warn him. More than that they wouldn't engage for; and Corporal Finch earnestly urged Charlie Samson to follow the same course.

But the drummer boy was already on his way, and somewhat sadly they watched him flicker among the trees, calling, 'Maddox! Maddox!' in a voice grown hoarse with despair.

Then suddenly the corporal stiffened. His great bony beak turned this way and that and his eyes glittered. He'd heard something else. He laid his enormous filthy finger to his lips. He nodded. 'They're coming!' he whispered. 'We'd best 'oof it bleedin' quick!'

The General's men were in the forest. As usual, Mister Shaw's prayers had not been answered. The god he believed in was far from almighty. Nothing had happened to deflect the General's two carriages. They had eaten up the dry and dusty miles like shining venomous insects and reached Burley soon after half past one.

Time and again the wretched fat man had offered to go into the forest alone and fetch out Fitzwarren. But General Lawrence wouldn't hear of it. He was too eager to shine before his glorious daughter as the ever youthful leader of armed men.

At last they halted at an inn too insignificant to have a name. An alarmed face stared at them through the tiny parlour window; then the proprietress – a Mrs Walsh – came out in a panic. She could offer nothing equal to the splendour and numbers of the company – not even Mr Walsh who was away from home.

But all the General wanted was a place where his daughter and her maid might rest after their journey. Sophia was tired, very tired . . .

Eagerly Mister Shaw offered again to go for Fitzwarren while the General attended his child. But now there turned out to be another reason against it. It seemed that Major Fitzwarren might panic and attack. He was dangerous. The General wouldn't hear of the surgeon exposing himself.

'Mark my words, sir,' said the General firmly. 'Fitzwarren

will defend himself. To the death. Armed men must go for him. And God forbid there should be an accident.'

'God forbid,' echoed Mister Shaw; but with no great conviction.

Something in the fat man's voice made the General glance at him sharply. For a moment they stared into each other's eyes. Each saw a frightened man – and neither really knew the reason why. But in that instant, each knew that the other would be driven to his very limits by that fear. Whatever the unlucky Mister Shaw might say or do, the General was going to have Fitzwarren shot down. Again and again the surgeon cursed himself for betraying the man; but in his heart of hearts he knew that he'd had no choice. His love for Charlie Samson touched both the best and the worst in him, and he was never sure which it was that tormented him the most.

Suddenly he remembered the survivors. The black clad servants would not stop to see who moved. They'd shoot down anything in red. Mister Shaw's frightened little eyes bulged at the primed muskets and the bland obedient faces of the General's men. Why should Finch die – or Parsons – or –?

'Shaw! Come back, sir! Shaw!'

But Mister Shaw had gone. He seemed to float and bounce off across the grass and into the shadowy trees like a large red ball that had been kicked by a child.

'After him!' shouted the General excitedly. 'Don't lose him! He'll lead us to Fitzwarren!' He waved gallantly to the parlour window from which Sophia was watching and from which came everything that sustained him in his murderous enterprise. 'The hunt is up!'

As she watched him go, Sophia's face was deathly white. There was fear in it, and anger, and something more besides.

Everywhere the drummer boy fancied he saw Maddox; in every bush and copse and vanishing across each clearing as he stumbled after. 'Maddox! Maddox! They're coming for you!'

Like a scarlet will o' the wisp, the image of Maddox danced

ahead of him, leading him deeper and deeper into the great forest.

Or *was* it Maddox? Was it perhaps the phantom of James Digby enmeshing him among the trees to drive him mad? The drummer boy stopped and stared round in anguish. Here in the woods he knew so well his plight seemed a thousand times worse than ever before. All about him there lingered memories of the love that must have brought him into the world. Now into the green and gold that tapestried the air he himself had woven the black threads of perjury and betrayal. There was little left for Charlie Samson, and he wished with all his heart that he'd fallen on the hillside – and so kept his shine in others' hearts. His haunted love for Sophia Lawrence still held him, but its chains were beginning to tear and wrench. 'Maddox! Maddox . . .'

He staggered on, but his voice was worn to a whisper. Then he saw Maddox. He was skirting a clearing and making for a group of trees that Charlie knew as Dames Wood. He had not seen the drummer boy. He was intent on where he was going. He was carrying what seemed to be a bucket of water.

For a few moments the boy followed him. He was quite oblivious to every sound, so fixed was he in the task of carrying the bucket without spilling it. It was as if his very soul depended on it.

Suddenly the boy saw he was making towards a gypsy's hut, 'Mrs Thompson!' Maddox called softly. 'I'm back. It's your friend, Mr Bruton . . .'

Charlie halted in astonishment. An ancient gypsy had hobbled out of the hut. A little scarf of smoke from her pipe wreathed itself across her dried-up cheeks. 'God bless you, Mr Bruton,' she mumbled as Maddox carried the bucket into her hut. 'And may you keep upright all your days.'

Maddox smiled. 'I'll come again tomorrow, ma'am. I'll –'

He stopped. There was a sound of someone running, heavily, rapidly.

Fearfully he looked round. He saw the drummer boy stand-

ing and watching him. His eyes filled up with their old terror. 'You're back!'

'Maddox! They're coming for you –'

'You betrayed me! I knew you would! I knew it – Oh God is there no escape for me?'

The sound of running came nearer. Maddox seemed unable to move.

'Maddox! Run – run for your life!' But still he could not move.

'Maddox!' Out of the trees, his coat ripped by passage through bush and thicket till his linen burst out like stuffing,

stumbled Mister Shaw. 'Thank God I've found you! They're coming, man! Run – run!'

Maddox glared from the surgeon to the drummer boy. 'Where can I run to? Where – where is there left for me?'

He took a few steps first one way, then the other. But could not make up his mind. He was too terrified to escape. He'd heard other sounds. Faintly, faintly came voices shouting . . . 'This way. Spread out. We've got him now!'

The drummer boy looked at the trembling surgeon with hatred. 'You brought them –'

'I – I –' squealed Mister Shaw, when suddenly it was

realized that Maddox was at last moving. The ancient gypsy had seized him. She was pushing him with all her strength, pushing him away towards Dames Wood. 'Run!' she screeched. 'And may the spirits of the forest watch over you!'

'There he goes!' The General's men had seen him. Only a glimpse, but it had been enough. The crazy old gypsy had pushed him the wrong way. Her long life had robbed her of her best faculties. The forest echoes had confused her. The General's men were coming through Dames Wood.

Black as night in their mourning livery, they moved among the trees. They were going to murder him.

'Spread out. Outflank him. We've got him!' The General's voice was brazen with triumph and joy.

'This way! He's run this way! Follow me –'

It was Mister Shaw's voice, shrieking desperately; but the General was not deceived. His dark regiment turned from the useless fat man and began to encircle their prey. Muskets were lifted for the first sure glimpse . . .

The wood rustled and quivered as if the troubled phantom of the dame whose name it bore would draw her skirts away from the hunted creature who clung to her for sanctuary.

The forest itself was turning against him and would betray him – even as the golden drummer boy had done. They were everywhere: all around him. Maddox fancied he glimpsed muskets dappled in the splintered sunlight. Were they going to kill him now? No – no! It was all in his mind. These were but the phantoms of the men whose lives he'd lost. He must go to them and plead for their forgiveness. Ten thousand forgivings . . .

Dazedly he began to creep towards them, when a terrible sound filled the air! The Retreat! A drum was thundering, roaring, menacing the air! He stopped. Where was the drum? It echoed and echoed from every corner of the wood. He clapped his hands to his ears and began to run and run.

The General's men had faltered. The drum had startled

them. Angrily the General was shouting, putting the fear of God into them. But his words were indistinct. The Retreat was drowning them. The black figures were wavering, turning this way and that. Drum seemed to be answering drum in the mysterious shaking air.

The drummer boy – the drummer boy! In and among the trees he stalked, drumsticks lifting high with a haughtiness that could never last. He was all but at the end of his road. He longed for his life to finish here where it had begun. All he prayed was that he might undo what he'd done and leave the world without the stain of having lived on it.

Suddenly a musket exploded. There was a cry of pain. Charlie Samson stopped drumming. The echoes died. Men were running, panting eagerly. 'Quick! Quick! He's wounded! May be dangerous. Shoot again. Finish him off!'

The drummer boy's heart turned to stone. But no second shot came. Instead, there was a screaming. A woman's voice. A woman running and stumbling and shouting and screaming for General Lawrence. It was Charity.

'Miss Sophia! Please – come quickly! I – I think she's dying!

15

IT had happened so quickly, like a candle suddenly guttering. Absolutely no warning. She'd fallen – and could not get up. She'd been quite well before. Even angry that the hunt had gone forward without her. Then – then Charity frowned as if unable to believe that Death could be so casual in his calling.

She was lying on a bench against the wall, supported with pillows. Mrs Walsh had done what she could to make her easy, but her establishment was too poor to run to much; and Mr Walsh was from home.

She'd not thought it wise to move the young lady upstairs – she'd not proper help. She'd offered a little brandy, but the young lady had not been equal to taking it. A pity. Brandy was a good thing; real French brandy . . . but customed, you understand. If only Mr Walsh had been home . . . But now, thank God, everyone was come.

Gratefully Mrs Walsh withdrew. The air was so heavy, so sweet, and the young lady frightened her. She went upstairs and left her parlour to the pale and distraught visitors.

Despite first Mrs Walsh's and now Charity's efforts, it was not possible to keep Sophia well covered. She was hot – far too hot. It was air she needed, and then she'd be all right. Could no one see she was suffocating for lack of it?

Gently Charity wiped her mistress's brow free of sweat. Peevishly Sophia looked up; then her expression softened when she saw her splendid father and – and the drummer boy! How had he come there? No matter. She was wonderfully pleased to see him. But he was so torn and ragged – and he was crying, too. How foolish he looked, standing there with his great drum, and childish tears finding pale paths down his dirty cheeks! She glanced to her father to share in the joke.

'The surgeon – the surgeon!' muttered the General. 'Where is he?'

Mister Shaw had not appeared. Something had delayed him. Angrily the General stared through the window. The surgeon's place was here, on parade! How dared he be absent when his daughter had need of him?

He tiptoed about the little room, hardly daring to look at his beautiful child. He seemed quite dazed by the calamity that had overtaken him so far from his home. From time to time he peered at the drummer boy and sighed. The lad's face was an image of frozen despair.

Suddenly there was a stirring from the bench. Why couldn't that girl Charity get out of the way so he could see what his daughter wanted?

Ah! She wanted him. She was beckoning. He straightened his shoulders and went to her, but could not quite refrain from glancing round the room for the comfort of a mirror.

He knelt down with a gentle creaking of stays and lifted the hem of her red dress off the floor. Then he took Sophia's papery white hand and held it in his own like a fatal dispatch.

She smiled at him – and he smiled back. Their expressions were curiously alike; and for a moment it seemed as if there was a secret and oddly sinister game being played between them – this huge magnificent General and his wondrous dying child.

'Charlie Samson,' she breathed. 'Remember how we talked of my blossoming while you faded? Now it's changed about.' Indeed, it really seemed that with the coming of the drummer boy the girl had lost ground terribly. 'The strength is all yours, now . . . can you not manage a – a smile for me?'

Somewhat grotesquely the drummer boy did as he was asked and joined the General at her side.

Her face was white as bone; but her eyes still blazed at him. There was a spot of bright red on her bosom. Charlie stared at it in horror. Then it moved and flew away. It had been a ladybird, only mocking blood.

'Don't leave me again . . . I'm frightened, Charlie. Stay with me till –'

'I'll never leave you. Never, never!'

She sighed contentedly, then said she would like to sleep for a little while. She was very tired. But no one was to go. Just a little rest and then she'd be better again. But stay . . .

She closed her eyes, but between her lashes the merest fragment of fire still glimmered at the drummer boy, as if, even in sleep there was something within that was very, very watchful. She remained thus for several minutes and it seemed that she was very likely to die on each breath.

But this sleep, if sleep it was, seemed to recover her a little – and so prolong the anguish of the watchers. She opened her eyes again. There was a troubled look in them.

'I – I dreamed,' she whispered. 'I dreamed that you had all gone and left me in a dark place. I dreamed I was all alone on our hillside, Charlie. I could hear your drum . . . but I could not find you. I ran and ran, but always you moved farther away. It was so cold there. The wind was sharp and bitter. It cut my skin and wrinkled it all over and I was like an old, old woman. I called to you . . . but only your drum answered, fainter, fainter . . . Come back to me, my drummer boy! Come back!'

'He's here, my darling,' muttered the General reassuringly. 'We're both here. We will not leave you, child.' He scowled as if at the cruelty with which life had turned on him. 'For her sake,' he whispered to the drummer boy, 'we must be brave, eh? She – she must not know anything. For her sake we must keep ourselves shining, eh? Not tarnish. Not be dishonoured . . . oh my dear boy!' He turned away, overcome; then he went on. 'For her sake, not for mine, you understand, we must clear ourselves. You understand? After all, what does anything else matter beside her? Her heart is so great. Her poor mother was so, exactly. Always, always for honour. What is life without it, eh? The hillside. You hear how she dreams of it? We must always keep it so. Not just ten thousand useless dead, but ten

thousand heroes we made for her that morning! A hundred thousand wouldn't have been too much! So – so your promise, my boy. Whatever happens, you will be on our – her side. Your promise . . . over my dying child!'

'I promise – I promise!' wept the drummer boy. He was stretched beyond all limits of endurance. How much longer –?

Suddenly Sophia's eyes widened. Had the moment come? 'Who is it?' she whispered. 'Who's there? Someone's come into the room!' There was fear in her eyes: even panic. 'No! No!'

But it proved to be no one worse than Mister Shaw. The fat man had come at last. He was panting from running and his mean little eyes blinked uneasily round the room. But the girl remained horribly agitated so that the General muttered to the surgeon that he'd best wait outside. There was no need for him now. He was too late . . . too late.

Too late for what? Mister Shaw peered at the drummer boy who was kneeling beside the General's daughter. Was he really too late? Was it always his fate to be too late? Was this the devil's mockery of the great gift he possessed – that he should never be able to use it? Battlefields . . . everywhere there were battlefields about which such lame souls as Mister Shaw limped and grubbed – too late.

'Go, my good fellow,' murmured the General again; and the surgeon felt the great man's hand on his shoulder. He shook himself free. His remarkably sharp eyes had been studying the pallid young woman on the bench. 'Please, don't you see how you distress her?' The General's voice had grown sharper as his daughter's dying eyes regarded the fat man with dread and hatred. It was as if she sensed that in his cold and avaricious heart there would be no pity for her.

'Go – go!' Now it was the drummer boy who implored him; and there was hatred in his eyes, too.

Mister Shaw shrugged his shoulders. He was accustomed to being disliked. He stepped with surprising neatness round the boy and bent down over the dying Sophia. This was his affair;

and no one could keep him from his trade. He laid his grimy hand on Sophia's white breast – then on the side of her neck. He touched her forehead, and peered into her eyes. An extraordinary look passed between the surgeon and the girl. Then Mister Shaw compressed his lips and drew back. He rubbed his hands together as if he'd touched something unwholesome.

'Come away, my dear,' he murmured to Charlie. 'No place for you here.'

The drummer boy looked at him in contempt. He shook his head; and Sophia smiled. 'Leave us,' muttered Charlie. 'Can't you see I must stay . . . stay till –'

'Till when?'

The boy remained silent. His expression was sufficient answer.

'Till when?' repeated Mister Shaw, as if determined to inflict all the pain he could.

'Till she dies,' breathed the boy with a terrible look.

'Then you'll stay a long time,' said Mister Shaw. 'She ain't even ill, my dear.'

Charlie Samson looked at him as if he was mad. What was the purpose of such a lie? Did he really fancy he'd be believed?

Mister Shaw frowned. He wasn't used to being doubted in the exercise of his trade. He turned to the General.

'*You* know she ain't dying,' he said. The General reddened angrily. He did not demean himself to answer the fat man.

The surgeon looked to Charity. She shook her head and he understood he could expect no help from her. She was in no situation to give it. Whatever his purpose, whether for good or ill, the odds against Mister Shaw were mounting. He began to breathe heavily and there was an angry, almost spiteful look in his eyes. 'But you know, don't you?' He spoke to Sophia herself. He stood directly over her. 'You know what you're about, don't you.'

She gazed up at him, as if not understanding. Painfully the drummer boy watched her. He did not dare drag Mister Shaw away for fear the commotion would do more damage than the fat man's ruthless words. He remembered how carefully the household had always shielded her.

'You know that the only sickness you have is more the priest's business than the physician's.'

Great tears had begun to well up in Sophia's eyes; but otherwise her expression remained unchanged. She did not understand . . .

Mister Shaw looked about him again. Plainly he was making little headway. The falling of Sophia's tears quite drowned out his little words.

So Mister Shaw raised his voice. He raised it till it filled the room with its shrill bleating. Sometimes his words were plain and calm; sometimes they were bitter and savage and cut like knives. The drummer boy could not keep them out, nor could he keep his eyes from the surgeon's flabby, painted face with its neat little mouth that opened and shut and opened and shut as if these words of his were in a devilish hurry to get out.

'You've come to such deathbeds before. Am I right – am I right? They're like marriage beds . . . but the lover must die. That's it, ain't it? It happens in nature, I know. Certain spiders, eh? Oh yes, nature can be quite as monstrous as men.' He looked hurriedly round the room as if for confirmation. 'It's possible there's an ecstasy in it . . . the spider, you know. But with you – with you it is a sickness. A malignant hysteria. Oh this is damnable!'

He turned on the drummer boy with such rapidity that Charlie could not avoid his eyes – and the boy seemed actually to stagger under the force of their expression. He put out his hand as if to steady himself against the deathbed. A wind seemed to be blowing at him – a freezing, bitter wind that stung and plucked and tore at the last golden thing he had left in the world: his love . . . his love . . .

But the fat man would not let him go. 'All my life, Charlie, I've walked in filth and blood and pain – and the smell of it is always in my nostrils. But here is a different stench. Here is the stink of corruption. Here is a hatred of life, a living from death to death! So – so she sits in her little room at the top of the house, quite shut away, feeding ... feeding ... The house fears her, dreads her; thus her malignant condition survives and flourishes. The father feeds her – and she feeds him. She feeds him on vanity; and he feeds her on death, endless, endless death –'

Stony amazement had seized the room, turning it into a mirror in which the fat man saw nothing but himself – an object of hatred and disgust. But he could not stop. He went on in a helpless panic, still seeking to reach a heart and mind that was shut fiercely against him. Thus his words became extreme and sometimes only caught at the fringes of his thoughts.

'Perhaps – perhaps she cannot help it? I don't know – I don't know. Perhaps the devil cannot help hating God? Perhaps, even, there's no hope for us and God must be destroyed? But – *but I will not stand by and watch it happen*!' He was panting and sweating under the fierceness of the passion that had seized hold of him.

'Can't you see that she's mocking life even as she's mocking death? Can't you see that – that all the gorgeous flags and banners and pennants are no better than – than tablecloths for her to feed off? And with what hellish appetite! Only a general could satisfy it! Monsters! They are monsters, Charlie –'

He wiped his brow on his sleeve and left a grimy furrow that seemed to give him a scowl of terrific proportions.

But the girl still gazed up at him calmly. It seemed there was no rage on earth that could shake her. She was beyond all reach. She lay amid her pillows like a fallen flower. Against such fragile beauty the surgeon understood his words were as nothing. He stammered, stuttered, then with that odd rapidity that always marked certain of his actions, he seized her by the shoulder. His movement had been too unexpected to be forestalled. He dragged at her till she sat upright. 'There!' he panted.

For an instant her face turned savagely on him. It was filled with wild hate. The drummer boy saw it. His heart thundered, but he clung all the more desperately to save this last of his visions from falling into ruin and decay. He looked again, and Sophia's head had lolled on her neck like a doll's and she'd sunk piteously away.

The General reached to grasp the fat man; but before he could, the drummer boy had struck the surgeon across the face.

'For the love of God, will you go?'

Mister Shaw staggered. He touched his cheek which was reddening worse than his rouge. Then his little eyes blazed up in a fury. 'How dare you strike me!' he squealed. 'How dare you speak of love and God!' He was quite transported with anger and he let loose the bitterness in his broken heart. 'Talk of love and God when you've seen the pain of the world. When you've seen men die of plague and little children starve. When you've seen husbands and fathers and sons hack and burn and hang each other in their millions . . . while bloody-hearted scoundrels ponder how to save their faces – and argue who to blame! *Then* talk of love and God and I'll listen!'

'Atheist! Blasphemer!' shouted the General in sudden triumph as at last a portion of the surgeon's outburst reached his military brain. 'Love is an abomination in your mouth, sir! You – you would destroy everything that's honourable and fine! But thank God we've found you out in time! Oh, we know your sort that loves neither honour nor country and would drag us all down! Thank God, I say, that out of your own mouth you've destroyed yourself! See! See! This golden lad shrinks from you!'

Mister Shaw looked. Charlie Samson was indeed shrinking away from him – as a child before a thunderstorm. The surgeon's bubble of rage was pricked. He opened and shut his mouth but no more words came. The drummer boy watched him fiercely.

'Atheist?' muttered Mister Shaw, seeming to be quite bewildered as to how and where he was. 'Blasphemer? No . . . no. I believe in a God, sir; but I must believe in a devil, too . . .

you understand . . . otherwise how could I endure it? But I do not always know which is which, sir . . .'

Contemptuously the General pushed past him. 'My child,' he murmured to his daughter who still gazed at the surgeon as if fascinated by him. 'All will be well. Our boy has promised, you know. His word means something. No dishonour, my dear . . . all will be as it should be . . . as it always was.' He extended an arm and encompassed the drummer boy who made no effort to escape.

But Charlie Samson was much shaken. Though Mister Shaw was not a good man – even a mean and greedy one – Charlie knew in his heart of hearts that Mister Shaw had a great talent and he would not willingly betray it. Such honour as he had left was in his genius; it was all he had to sustain him. It was when the drummer boy had seen the brief look of fear and hatred in Sophia's eyes that he'd felt himself topple. But such love as Charlie's was not rooted out so quickly. He still saw himself in her matchless eyes. He saw himself reflected as the shining drummer boy who would not tarnish or change. This was a strong image and not to be cast aside. It was stronger, far stronger than the fat man's fury.

'My drummer boy,' whispered Sophia, and touched his hand with hers. Her skin was as cold and fierce as ice.

'I'll make it worth your while,' said the General.

'And so will I, my drummer boy.'

'Promotion,' added the General, his blue eyes twinkling amiably.

'Goodbye, Mister Shaw.'

Charity had spoken. Her voice was quiet and respectful. Nothing more. The torn and defeated fat man had shuffled unnoticed to the door. Now, arrested by Charity's words, he paused and looked back at the drummer boy and at all the fine hopes he himself had dashed aside.

'Forgive me,' he mumbled, 'but, in my way, I loved you dearly, Charlie Samson. I loved you well enough to hurt you and even to part from you. I loved you because – because you seemed to me the real spirit of life and hope . . . Such as you, Charlie Samson, can keep a heaven over our heads with your word; and – and lead some of us out of hell. I watched you – watched you leave the battlefield with your dreams; and you were very bright and shining. I was almost frightened of you, Charlie; you dazzled wherever you walked. But now – but now your shine has almost gone and your poor little light will just last out to see this dreadful pair safely to their home. Yes. Your word will be taken at the court martial and the dead weight of ten thousand lives will be shifted from one man's door to another's. But thereafter, Charlie, there will be nothing left of you, and wherever you go, there will be darkness. Good-bye, Charlie Samson.'

He left the room. Charlie felt the General's arm tighten round his shoulder, and Sophia's hand grip his own. He was secured. He looked at them. They were both watching him – and nodding. Sophia's face was flushed now; the pallor had quite gone. She looked more lovely than ever . . . and her lips were resistlessly curving in a triumphant smile. He turned away. He was frightened and confused.

Suddenly the love of the unhappy fat man seemed no little thing. He faltered. He looked to Charity. Her eyes were else-where and her curiously pretty face betrayed nothing. She would not look at him and cast her weight into the scales. Why would she not help him? He needed her. He was quite alone.

Miserably he stared to the window. Mister Shaw was sham-bling across a patch of grass. His shoulders looked more bent than ever – as if his back had been broken under a great weight. He kept glancing sideways as if, against all hope, there was someone walking by his side. Then he'd shake his head. Farther and farther he went – and Charlie Samson felt his loneliness like a knife in his own heart.

He looked back to the General and Sophia. Their smiles were unchanged – but they seemed to the boy like strangers. Their features no longer made sense, nor reminded him of anything. The great scarlet General and his lovely daughter . . . what did they want with him?

Suddenly they were in his way. They were in the way of the world! An obscure and breathless anger filled him. He pushed them aside.

'Mister Shaw!' he shouted at the top of his voice. 'I ain't going to light nobody home and let the heavens fall! Wait for me, Mister Shaw! I'm coming, sir –'

Charity's eyes were gleaming like stars.

16

MADDOX had escaped – got clean away and vanished as if off the face of the earth. The man who'd been shot was someone else altogether. Not a grievous wound – only in the fleshy part of the leg and Mister Shaw had tended it. It was the rosy-cheeked aide. His genius for getting in the way had extended even to a bullet. He had not had a good day.

But he was better received than he expected. General Lawrence was very affable. Refused to blame him for getting shot. Even sat him in the coach beside his extraordinarily beautiful daughter. Though desperately ill, Miss Lawrence contrived to smile at him. He'd never before seen anything so heart-breakingly lovely . . .

'Fitzwarren,' murmured the General. 'You saw him run from us? Confession of guilt, eh? You saw! You'll testify?'

'I – I –'

But the General hushed him. Speak of it later. His child wasn't strong . . . must be careful . . . must protect her at all costs. After all, what could anything signify beside such a dream of lovely youth dying in its prime? Gently . . . gently . . . they say she's not long for this world, my boy . . .

For several minutes the surgeon and the drummer boy walked in silence through the trees. Then Charlie discovered they were going the wrong way. They turned about and walked back. Presently, Mr Walsh's inn stood across the grass before them. The General's carriages were gone. Charlie sighed. 'Left something behind,' he said awkwardly. 'Mind if I fetch it?'

Mister Shaw nodded and attempted to push the stuffing back inside his coat. The parlour windows were open and, as they passed them, a faint sweetness still lingered in the air. They went inside.

'I fancied you'd be back for it.'

A young woman was sitting in the parlour, stitching at the hem of her black gown that the forest had unkindly torn. It was Charity. She smiled ruefully at the drummer boy, then bent to nibble at the thread.

'I – I thought you'd gone,' stammered Charlie, picking up the drum he'd gone off without.

She glanced up. 'I think we're both out of a job, thanks to your fat friend.' But to be honest, she did not look sorry about it and it seemed that the parting had been more the work of her heart than her head.

Mister Shaw fidgeted, mumbled an apology, which Charity brushed aside. She held out her needle and thread. 'Here,' she said. 'Stitching's in your line, they say. Me petticoat needs a daintier hand than mine.'

So Mister Shaw knelt down with a further splitting of his coat and set to work on Charity's impudent petticoat, the frill of which languished apart. Charlie watched him with a mixture of amusement and annoyance when a remarkable thing happened.

A head came round the door. A smallish, seamy, uneasy head. 'It's only them,' said Charity. The head nodded and proved to be attached to a very warlike figure. A soldier with an injured arm. Private Edwards. He was followed by Mrs Walsh. He saluted Charlie, then went to sit beside Charity.

It turned out that Private Edwards, full of Celtic charm, had got himself a comfortable billet till his arm should heal. He was quite one of the family . . . and much beloved of three little Walshes to whom he told great tales of battles far away. Nor was Mrs Walsh displeased when she saw her children crowding round the damaged soldier's knee. What with Mr Walsh being so often from home on Isaac Gulliver's business, it was a comfort to have a man about the house. And Private

Edwards further recommended himself by sometimes carrying out the dishes with his one good arm.

But now Private Edwards was treating Charity to the benefit of his Celtic charm and bravely making light of his injury.

Charlie stared at her, with Mister Shaw at her feet and Private Edwards at her side. He grew unreasonably irritated. He stalked towards the door. 'I'm off,' he said.

Mister Shaw snapped his thread and stood up. 'Where to?'

'On me way,' said Charlie coldly.

'Far to go?' Charity spoke. She was shaking out her gown and glancing approvingly at the way her repaired petticoat peeped out.

'Far enough,' said Charlie.

'Care for more company?'

He shrugged his shoulders. The world was wide; the world was free. Folk might go where they chose. Graciously he nodded – and stepped aside as Charity swept out before him.

With infinite caution the survivors once more emerged, each from their green and private shades. They stepped across a patch of sunlight and the great dusty beam rendered them vague and dreamlike as large red motes.

'Went the day well, young 'un?' asked Corporal Finch with a kindly smile. 'Did our arms prosper? Was we victorious, so to speak?'

Charlie Samson shrugged his shoulders.

'La gurr. La cruel gurr,' sighed the corporal, understanding more than might have been supposed. 'No victory without defeat, eh? All war's civil war, when all's said and done. It always turns out to be a brother we've so valorously done in. Even so, I'd 'ave been in there beside you, shoulder to shoulder, back to back and what-'ave-you, if me ankle 'ad been 'ealthy and sound. Mister Shaw! Dare I 'ope, sir, 'ave you remembered, sir, in a word, sir, 'ave you brung me gnashers?'

Then he saw Charity. She came from among the trees carefully holding up her skirts and smiling at nothing. The great bony corporal was enchanted – and harshly cut off a coarse remark grinning Parsons had begun.

But Mushoo, his French blood coursing through his French veins, turned irresistible. His neat little chest swelled, his black eyes took on a forgotten twinkle and a gallant smile lurked in the forests of his moustache. Suddenly he was more than a man: he was a Frenchman, and he set about captivating Charity with a cannonade of compliments that would have proved mortal had she understood a word of them.

Corporal Finch listened interestedly for a few moments, then gave up. The stream was too swift for any pickings. But Charlie Samson regarded Charity and Mushoo with great disfavour. He didn't blame the Frenchman. After all, it was only his nature. He blamed Charity. She was too free and easy in her manner for his liking. Too ready to be flattered; too encouraging.

He found himself becoming extraordinarily angry. It was high time he was on his way. Already the huge beam of sunlight had shifted and been split by lower branches. Already the scarlet figures were beginning to lose their colour as the forest deepened.

Then, quite suddenly, Mushoo fell silent. He stared. Corporal Finch who'd retired awhile with Mister Shaw, had rejoined them. Birdlike as ever, he advanced towards Charity with his hopping limp, snapping and flashing as he came. He was grinning. Indeed he could do very little else. His gnashers – his magnificent gnashers – were in. Mr Voice's masterpiece; and the pewter mouthplate gleamed under his long black lip like a coin stuck in a money-box. He stretched out a hand.

'Fwhinch,' he struggled to say. 'By wer grafe ow God a cohohal an' hurwiwing!'

Splendid as they were, Corporal Finch's fine French teeth had stretched his lines of communication till they'd all but snapped.

The huts the gypsies had abandoned stood at the edge of the clearing like three old men who'd sat down and refused to die. Bushes and grass had grown up about them, but they would not fall. And now they'd obtained a fresh lease on life. The survivors had been busy and Corporal Finch's office was fully furnished. From God knew where, he'd got a curtain, a bed, a scrap of carpet and a table. He was very proud of it all and was only sorry that there was room for no one else but himself inside.

He sat at his table regarding his companions outside with a gentle melancholy. The forest light had so gone down that he'd lit a candle which made his little home glow like a jewel with himself at the heart of it. His teeth glinted on a shelf behind him. There they were to stay, to be admired and treasured, but only to be used on the corporal's high days and holidays when appearances counted for more than words.

Mister Shaw was restless to be off. Already he'd shaken hands with Parsons and Mushoo. Now he did likewise with Corporal Finch across the table. The candle flickered and cast soft shadows across their faces. The corporal nodded sadly and the fat man frowned and smiled.

'Off to the wars, Mister Shaw?'

The surgeon nodded.

'May your arms prosper, Mister Shaw, sir. And may you partake of the fruits of victory at the banquet of la vee.'

In spite of himself, Mister Shaw smiled. The corporal's gleanings always opened up such fascinating conjectures as to what fields he must have wandered in.

He turned to go. His way lay towards Ringwood and the public coach. Silently he saluted Charity and then the drummer boy whose way lay elsewhere. To Charlie he'd said goodbye before; besides, he'd little time before the forest night. He began to walk away, waving once or twice as he went. Then he quickened his pace into a lively waddle. This was the last sight of him, with his bags of teeth hanging from his belt and his pale smudge of a flabby face peering from side to side as if nervous of lurking dragons. A very fat and greedy and reluctant knight errant who went his ways amid the mud and filth and pain of the world, not with a lance but a lancet.

Now it was Charlie's turn. His way lay farther to the east and north, even to Lyndhurst.

''Ome, lad?' murmured Corporal Finch. ''Ome from the wars?'

The drummer boy scowled and nodded. What else was there?

'Then give us a tune as you go, Charlie Samson; for that's 'ow first we met. Remember?'

So Charlie Samson began to walk; and as he walked he drummed softly while behind him the survivors with Charity still among them dwindled and flickered away as if into the phantoms and ghosts from which they'd first seemed to come. Nor did he stop his drumming when they were out of sight. Instead he beat louder and louder – as if determined that wherever he went in the dark forest someone should know which way to follow.

Furiously he thumped and banged a warlike Advance . . . advance . . . advance! His fists rose high above his head and the drumsticks struck like cannon balls. Advance – advance! The drum bellowed and groaned and quivered. And then, with a last uproarious roll, it rattled and died. He had split the drumskin!

He stared at it in abject dismay. Even that had left him. He laid it in the grass and knelt beside it. Then, little by little, he began to weep till his tears came fast and free. He wept for his broken drum; he wept for his dreams of Sophia Lawrence, and for the dreams of all such as he; he wept for the ten thousand scarlet men who slept on the hillside and would dream no more . . . Then he became aware there was someone by him. He looked up and fancied he saw a man in scarlet . . . a man with a broken head.

'Have you no tears for me?' whispered the ghost.

'Yes . . . yes! And for you too, James Digby. You most of all . . . you most of all!'

Then the ghost held out its insubstantial hand and seemed to rise in the darkling air. Charlie tried to touch it – to reach it; but it was dwindling fast. Up and up it went towards a small piece of sky between the trees. Early stars were visible . . . tiny pinpricks of light such as sometimes glinted on muskets and buttons. Now the ghost was but a faint patch, then a dot . . . till some wafting of light caught its buttons and it glinted briefly and was lost altogether among the faintest of the stars.

Now night has overtaken all the forest and the greater stars wink and glimmer among the high branches like jewelled berries. From time to time there is a sharp rustling as some secret creature moves from shadow to shadow, intent on its deep concerns.

Wearily and with many a rueful sniff, the drummer boy stands up and rubs his knees. It's high time he was on his way. He begins to walk – when something else moves more quickly than he.

Among the shades, a young woman has been standing and watching him for a long time.

'The drum, Charlie! Don't forget the drum!'

He turns, half startled out of his wits.

'Charity!'

He cannot prevent a smile that seems twice as wide as his face as he understands that his prayer was answered and that Charity followed the sound of the drum. Then he frowns as he realizes she must have witnessed his childish tears; and he remembers to be offended on account of her being too free and easy for his liking. But he cannot keep it up because Charity is standing very close to him.

'Your tinker,' he says wryly. 'D'you think I'll get a shilling for me drum now?'

She shakes her head gravely and sits down beside that military object. Her dark gown spreads and sighs and makes a stormy pool about her with her white petticoat foaming out of it like a tumbled wave. She holds out a hand and Charlie sits beside her.

He cannot see her face very clearly as it is shadowed by her unconfined hair. But her eyes have a very agreeable shine.

Gently she lays her hand on the ruined drum where it meets Charlie's. 'Would you part with it, Charlie? This drum that's gone thundering up the hillside while brave men fell and died all round you?'

'Me heart was thumping just as loud. I'll keep that instead.'

'And wasn't it the same drum that was played, slow and solemn, over the battle's dead?'

'It's been played in Wardour Street, too . . . for shillings at a time.'

Her hand advances over his and tightens. Her fingers are firm, but infinitely gentle. 'Let's keep the drum, Charlie. I can't imagine you without it.'

'Must I always be a drummer boy?'

'Oh yes. Even when you're an old, old man. There'll always be the ghost of the drummer boy in your heart – and in mine.'

'Do you believe in ghosts, Charity?'

'Such ghosts as that. We're all ghosts, I suppose. Even now, there's somewhere in you the ghost of that far-off grandfather. A sturdy old fellow –' She laughs. 'But a bit of a rogue when he gets the chance! A real old soldier though he's never seen a musket for fifty years or more! There he sits, in his high-backed chair before the fire and tells his grandchildren such a parcel of howling lies about his warlike deeds that their little ears stick out and their hair stands straight on end! Then they'll see the drum, sitting on the other side of the fire. 'Is that the very drum, Grandpapa?' they'll ask. And you'll nod and tell them all over again. And perhaps old Charity will come in from the kitchen and go to the drum (for, since it's got no drumskin, she likes to keep vegetables in it). She'll look at you and maybe listen. Yes, I'm sure she'll listen – though she's heard it all a thousand times before – and she'll look into your eyes for the ghost of the drummer boy . . . and – and the time when he broke his drum.'

'Am I – am I a ghost then, Charity?'

His hand has turned so that now their fingers are entwined. 'And are you a ghost?' His voice is no more than a whisper among whispers, for her mysteriously pretty face is very close to his.

'Me?' she chuckles. 'Oh no, Charlie! I'm just a special Charity for drummer boys!'

Suddenly her smile seems to fill the forest and the night . . . so Charlie Samson shuts his eyes and kisses it . . .

Their eyes have become accustomed to the dark and the great trees give up their intricate details. Here an oak, once struck perhaps by lightning, has opened up its heart from which is growing a sinewy nest of roots, looking so like a pattern of serpents that it seems that nature has turned sculptor and copied herself in wood. Indeed, everywhere can be seen this natural commentary as Charity and Charlie gaze wide-eyed about them. Bushes turn into patient, watchful does and the upper air is full of the proud, branching antlers of leaping stags.

'Where are we, Charlie?'

'It's called Knightswood Oak.'

'Was there a knight, then?'

Charlie thinks; then he remembers something and smiles. It is a very happy, almost mischievous smile that puzzles Charity not a little.

'As me father would say, it's believed there *was* a knight. One Sir William who was mistook for a deer and kippered with an arrow on this very spot.'

'William?' murmurs Charity. 'William. That's a fine name . . .'

Slowly they climb to their feet. It's high time they were on their way. The drum. They laugh and pick it up and carry it between them out of Knightswood Oak.

Much, much farther to the north, a shadowy figure leaves the forest. It runs as if pursued or pursuing. It is Fitzwarren – or Maddox – or Bruton. Now he vanishes once more into the darkness of remoter countrysides. Where is he going, this haunted man? Nobody knows and he is not heard of more. But – one day, perhaps – in a village in distant Derbyshire they will talk of a tall, gaunt stranger who was with them for a while, worked his fingers to the bone among the needy and the sick, then vanished as if off the face of the earth. They knew him as a Mr Berkeley who much resembled a Mr Bond who toiled similarly in Yorkshire – and a Mr Piccadilly in Durham.

Indeed if these shadowy figures who bore the names of so many London streets were one and the same, it would seem that this man was fixed on saving at least ten thousand lives. Could it be Maddox who has discovered at last that while death does not improve a coward or make wise a fool, there's always a chance that life might?

But now through the dark quiet streets of Lyndhurst walk the drummer boy and his girl. The journey has been farther than they supposed and they are both very tired. At last they come to a fine old inn. They pause in front of it and read the sign. *The Doe's Rest. W Samson, Proprietor.* Charlie Samson nods and smiles and Charity looks briefly nervous but then is reassured.

Charlie knocks on the door, then steps aside and waits. There are sounds from within. He looks proudly into his girl's eyes. At last the drummer boy has come home from the wars, with Charity on his arm – and charity deep in his heart.

THE END

ABOUT THE AUTHOR

Leon Garfield was born in Brighton, Sussex, in 1921. His brief art studies were interrupted by the outbreak of World War II, when he joined the Army and served in the Medical Corps for five years. In Belgium he met his artist wife, who suggested that he would do better as a writer.

After the war he worked as a bio-chemist until his success as an author allowed him to devote himself to writing full-time. His first published book, *Jack Holborn*,* won the Boys' Clubs of America Junior Book Award. His second, *Devil-in-the-Fog*,* won the Manchester Guardian Award for Children's Fiction in 1967. His third, *Smith** won the Arts Council prize of 1969: Best Book for Older Children Published in 1966–68. Both *Smith* and *Devil-in-the-Fog* were serialized on television. His latest books to appear in Puffins were *Black Jack* and *Mister Corbett's Ghost*.

Leon Garfield and his wife have one daughter, Jane, and three cats: George, a red Persian tabby; Fudge, a blue Persian; and Abbey, an Abyssinian. He also has an Old English sheepdog called Henry.

* *All available in Puffins*

Some other Peacocks

GENERAL

ESPECIALLY FOR GIRLS

Louisa M. Alcott *Good Wives*
Enid Bagnold *National Velvet*
Beverly Cleary *Fifteen*
Esther Hautzig *The Endless Steppe*
Janet Hitchman *King of the Barbareens*
Grace Allen Hogarth *As a May Morning*
Irene Hunt *Up a Road Slowly*
Margaret Kennedy *The Constant Nymph*
James Vance Marshall *Walkabout*
L. M. Montgomery *Anne of Green Gables*
Dodie Smith *I Capture the Castle*
William Stevenson *The Bushbabies*

Some Penguins you might enjoy

Alain Fournier   *Le Grand Meaulnes*
Kingsley Amis   *Lucky Jim*
Stan Barstow   *A Kind of Loving*
Max Beerbohm   *Zuleika Dobson*
G. K. Chesterton *The Man who was Thursday*
Joseph Conrad   *Lord Jim*
John Christopher   *The World in Winter*
Monica Dickens   *One Pair of Feet*
Monica Dickens *One Pair of Hands*
Monica Dickens *My Turn to make the Tea*
Gerald Durrell   *My Family and other Animals*
C. S. Forester   *The African Queen*
E. M. Forster   *A Passage to India*
Thor Heyerdahl   *The Kon-Tiki Expedition*
Jerome K. Jerome   *Three Men in a Boat*
Aldous Huxley   *Brave New World*
Richard Hughes   *A High Wind in Jamaica*

Some Penguins you might enjoy

Ernest Hemingway   *For Whom the Bell Tolls*

Barry Hines   *A Kestrel for a Knave*

Compton Mackenzie   *Whisky Galore*

Thomas Mann   *Buddenbrooks*

Laurie Lee   *Cider with Rosie*

Laurie Lee   *As I walked out one Midsummer Morning*

W. Somerset Maugham   *Of Human Bondage*

Alan Moorehead   *No Room in the Ark*

W. C. Sellar and R. J. Yeatman   *1066 and All That*

George Orwell   *Animal Farm*

Alan Paton   *Cry the Beloved Country*

Françoise Sagan   *Bonjour Tristesse*

Muriel Spark   *The Prime of Miss Jean Brodie*

Josephine Tey   *The Daughter of Time*

John Steinbeck   *The Grapes of Wrath*

Keith Waterhouse   *Billy Liar*

Oscar Wilde   *The Picture of Dorian Gray*

John Wyndham   *The Midwich Cuckoos*

Sandy Wilson   *The Boy Friend*